'So what did  **you?' Greg a**

'It's confidential.'

'But she's my patient. We should make some record of it.'

'No, we shouldn't. There are times when we have to keep secrets and this is one of them.'

'Lindy, look at me.' He put his hand on her arm, forcing her to stop. 'If we're to work together, we mustn't have secrets we don't share,' he said firmly.

She caught her breath and then realised that he was still referring to their patient. How could he know about her own secret. . .their secret?

Margaret Barker pursued a variety of interesting careers before she became a full-time author. Besides holding a BA degree in French and Linguistics, she is a Licentiate of the Royal Academy of Music, a State Registered Nurse and a qualified teacher. Happily married, she has two sons, a daughter and an increasing number of grandchildren. She lives with her husband in a sixteenth-century thatched house near the East Anglian coast.

Recent titles by the same author:

NEVER SAY NEVER
IMPOSSIBLE SECRET
LAKESIDE HOSPITAL
THE DOCTOR'S DAUGHTER
SURGEON'S DILEMMA

LOVED AND LOST

BY
MARGARET BARKER

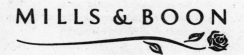

*MILLS & BOON, the Rose Device and
LOVE ON CALL are trademarks of the publisher.
Harlequin Mills & Boon Limited,
Eton House, 18-24 Paradise Road, Richmond, Surrey TW9 1SR*

© Margaret Barker 1996

ISBN 0 263 79543 8

*Set in Times 10 on 11 pt. by
Rowland Phototypesetting Limited
Bury St Edmunds, Suffolk*

03-9605-49822

*Made and printed in Great Britain
Cover illustration by Simon Bishop*

CHAPTER ONE

LINDY could feel the colour draining from her face. She took a deep breath to steady her nerves as she listened to her boss.

'Lindy, this is Dr Greg Dalton, our new specialist in infertility treatment. He's going to take charge of our clinic so that I can keep my work going in obstetrics,' Bradley Prestcot was saying in a matter-of-fact tone of voice. 'Greg, this is Dr Lindy Cash, our junior house surgeon.'

Lindy was vaguely aware of her consultant's voice continuing as he outlined why she'd been chosen to work in the new infertility clinic at Moortown General Hospital. Brad was explaining to the new man how Lindy had done a four-week induction course to give her an insight into what was needed at the clinic, that she was also following a programme of in-service training in infertility, and that she would be spending some of her time doing her normal work as a junior house surgeon in the obstetrics and gynaecology department.

Lindy's concentration was wavering. The thought that Brad expected her to work with Greg Dalton, the man she'd avoided for nearly two years, was too much for her to swallow.

'How do you do, Dr Cash?'

She heard Greg's voice as if in a dream. He was even holding out his hand towards her—that broad, long-fingered, dark, hair-covered hand she remembered so well. The sardonic smile on his face seemed to be mocking her; she was sure that he was

5

enjoying her discomfiture. It was her worst nightmare come true.

'No need for introductions, Brad,' Greg was saying. 'Lindy and I have already met.'

She held out her hand, wincing as Greg's fingers wrapped themselves around hers in a vice-like grip.

'I thought Robert Vincent had been appointed to take charge here,' she said quietly, pulling away her hand, curling up her fingers by her side as if she'd been stung by a wasp.

'Ah, let me explain,' Greg said quickly.

Lindy raised her green eyes to his and averted them almost immediately, running a hand nervously through her long red hair. He was still smiling, damn him! How could he be so insensitive? Didn't he realise that she couldn't possibly work with him?

'Robert Vincent was first choice for this post but he dropped out at the last minute,' Greg explained in that deep, husky voice she'd once found so sexy. 'When Brad phoned me yesterday I got special permission to leave my position as second in command of an infertility unit in London. The powers that be knew that I'd been short-listed for this post and might have to leave at short notice.'

'You may as well know,' Brad put in, 'that you were my first choice all along, Greg. The board of governors outnumbered me in votes for the simple reason that most of the old dinosaurs thought that, being only thirty-two, you were too young to handle this position. But I've heard excellent reports of your work in London and I felt you were the man for the job. So, how do you come to know Lindy?'

Lindy was squirming inwardly. 'We trained at the same hospital,' she said from between clenched teeth. Raising her eyes again, she forced herself to meet Greg's. Those brown eyes she remembered so well, that dark, shiny hair, considered by some members of the medical profession to be too long for a doctor in a responsible position. That would be one reason why the board of ancient governors hadn't chosen him. And maybe they took exception to the kink in his misshapen nose. It gave him the appearance of a boxer.

She found herself having to suppress an involuntary shiver as she remembered running her finger along it whilst Greg had told her that he'd had an argument with a huge Welsh forward on the rugby field when he was still at school.

Brad was watching her quizzically. 'So, you know each other quite well?'

'No,' Lindy said emphatically.

'Yes,' Greg said simultaneously, his devil-may-care smile broadening on his face.

'We've never worked together,' Lindy put in hastily. The strain and embarrassment of this unexpected situation was becoming unbearable. She could feel the colour rising in her cheeks as the poignant memories flooded back. 'We met once. . .very briefly. Look, I really must get back to the obstetrics department. I have patients to see on Nightingale Ward and—'

'Lindy, I've cleared you for the whole morning,' Brad interrupted, his frown deepening. 'Greg needs your help with the infertility outpatient clinic. I've got a long morning in theatre so I can't come over till this afternoon. Are you feeling OK?'

'Fine!' she lied as she played for time. How on earth was she going to cope? She would have to get Brad on his own and explain that she couldn't possibly work in the infertility clinic when Greg was in charge. 'I just thought. . .'

Her voice trailed away as she realised that she couldn't back out at the beginning of the clinic. She had to work through the morning and then sort something out with Brad this afternoon.

She willed herself to look up at Greg. 'Right; let's get started.'

Her legs felt weak and wobbly as she moved out of Greg's consulting room and across the narrow corridor. Her name was already on the door opposite. She pushed it open.

'Rona! Am I glad to see you!' she told the staff nurse who was sorting through a pile of case notes.

Rona Phillips grinned. 'Nice to be appreciated. But why me in particular?'

'You're a familiar face—someone from obstetrics. I'm glad you asked to come and work over here. That four-week induction course last month was pretty intense but it's all so new and I'm still learning on the job.' Lindy sank down onto her chair and switched on the computer.

'You were lucky to be chosen to work here. It's a good career move.'

'Yes, I certainly thought so, but now. . .'

'But now, what, Lindy?' Rona asked, her face registering the concern she felt at the sudden apparent personality change in one of her favourite doctors. 'You're usually so full of beans. Has something happened to upset you? I mean you were so looking forward to working with the new specialist.'

'That's just the point. I thought Robert Vincent was coming here. Apparently he dropped out at the last minute and—'

She broke off as the door opened. The huge frame of her rugby-playing, boxer-look-alike new boss filled the doorway. She heard Rona's involuntary gasp and surmised that her staff nurse was probably experiencing that instant attraction that the wretched man exerted over gullible young women.

'Yes, I'm sorry you'll have to put up with me, Lindy,'

Greg Dalton told her evenly. 'Must be quite a let-down when you were expecting the eminent Dr Vincent.'

'It is,' Lindy said, her steely calm expression belying her inner emotional turmoil.

Rona Phillips grabbed the list of patients from Lindy's desk and headed for the waiting room, muttering something incoherent. She glanced nervously at the newcomer as she ducked under his arm, and was rewarded with a brilliant smile, which displayed perfect white teeth that had somehow survived the rigours of his athletic youth.

Lindy held her breath as Greg moved into the room with the easy grace of a panther stalking its prey. The door closed. They were alone. She wasn't so much nervous as terrified.

'Long time no see,' he said, leaning against the examination couch, his eyes fixed on her face. 'I gather from Bradley Prestcot that you asked to specialise in infertility when he started up the clinic in November. For the past two months you've been attending seminars, including an intensive course last month. It would be a shame if I were to waste all that time and money by asking for a replacement doctor, but I warn you, Lindy, if you don't behave like a total professional I'll have you out of here so quick you'll—'

'And I warn you, Greg, I've no intention of staying now that you're here. I can easily get another job in an infertility clinic or I can go back to full-time obstetrics. So, I'll go now if you like.'

She stood up, trembling with anger, her hands flailing around the desk in inconsequential movements, gathering up the case notes, picking up pens and pencils. How dared he speak to her like that?

'Don't you think you're being rather childish?' he said quietly, moving suddenly so that he was towering above her.

She leaned back against the desk, feeling his breath fanning her face. She would only have to move her hand and she could touch him. Greg, the mythical man of her dreams, or rather the man of her nightmares, was here in the flesh. Twenty-two months ago she'd hoped she would never see him again.

He reached forward and put his hands on either side of her shoulders. She tensed at the feel of fingers that threatened to evoke the painful memories that she'd successfully blotted out for so long. She fought to stay in control of her emotions. She mustn't break down in front of him.

'Take your hands off me,' she said calmly. 'I'm certainly not being childish. We both know we can't work together so the sooner we. . .'

'You can't walk out and leave me high and dry on my first morning here,' Greg said firmly, moving away to stand with his back towards her as he appeared to study the view from her consulting-room window.

Lindy looked across the room. The muscles of Greg's broad back were straining the seams of his dark grey suit. She'd never seen him in a suit before. The dark hair reached over his impeccably white, beautifully ironed shirt collar. His wife was obviously clever with the laundry, but not clever enough to keep tabs on her cheating husband.

Beyond the bulky frame outlined in the pale morning sunlight, Lindy could see the rest of the snow-covered buildings that composed the recently erected infertility clinic annexe. In the distance, over the urban rooftops, the wintry white hills surrounding Moortown were in a state of sleepy hibernation. Nothing happened up there in winter. The sheep huddled together for warmth close to the farms; even the cows were reluctant to leave the warmth of the byre when milking was over.

It was only January—still three months to go before she completed her year as junior house surgeon. It wouldn't look good if she abandoned ship now, she thought. It would be stupid to jeopardise a career that meant everything to her. Better toe the line till April at any rate. After that she could please herself. But could she be professional for three months with the man who'd caused her such misery?

She took a deep breath to steady her nerves. 'Tell you what, Greg,' she said slowly. 'I need this job. I'm not going to sacrifice my career for you, or anybody else for that matter. So you can have my professional support here. We can behave as if we've never met before. Bury the past.'

He swung around. 'Fine. Let's not waste any more time.' The relief on his face was patently obvious. 'I want you to spend the morning in my consulting room so that you can find out how I work.'

Lindy frowned as she glanced at the pile of case notes on her desk. 'But I've got all these patients to see. If—'

'We'll see them together in my room,' he told her in a firm, no-nonsense voice.

'It will take too long,' Lindy pointed out.

'Who's in charge here?' he asked with icy calm.

She swallowed hard. What an infuriating man! 'No need to pull rank on me, Greg. It's OK; I'll do whatever you say to keep the professional peace.'

With a determined effort she forced herself to concentrate on the task in hand as she heard Greg leaving. She told herself that the past was over and done with; the future was all that mattered.

There was no doubt about it, she thought, feeling a sense of professional calm descending as she gathered up her case notes and switched off the computer; the clinic had proved very popular in the three months that it had been open.

Brad had started it up in the obstetrics outpatients in November, but now that the rapidly erected annexe was open they were able to see patients in purpose-built consulting rooms. They still had to use the path lab and operating theatres in the main building of the hospital, but eventually an operating theatre would be added and they would be totally independent.

She'd been so excited about her new work here, so keen to learn everything she could about the infertility programme that she was involved with.

She took a deep breath as she tapped on Greg's door, telling herself she had to control her emotions for the sake of the patients and her own career.

Greg had placed two chairs in front of his desk— one at either end. He motioned to her to sit down on one of them, taking the case notes from her and placing them on the desk.

In the corner of the room was Grace Brown, his newly appointed secretary, sitting in front of a computer, poised for action. Lindy had known Grace when she'd been a temporary medical secretary in Obstetrics. During the last couple of months, when Grace had worked in the infertility department, Lindy had found her extremely hardworking and capable.

'Grace is going to keep the records. You and I are going to listen to the patients. That's the way I like to work, Lindy. Eye contact, hands on, get to know the patients; don't intimidate them by sitting scribbling or tapping behind a desk.

'It takes courage for a couple to come in here and ask for help in getting pregnant. Some of them have suffered enough already, and the last thing they need is some unknown doctor starting to pontificate and talk gobbledegook when all they really want is a friend who understands their problem. I don't know what sort of approach Bradley Prestcot takes but—'

'Brad is extremely friendly and helpful with the patients,' Lindy put in. 'And I've learned a great deal about infertility treatment in the last three months. My work in obstetrics and gynaecology isn't totally alien to this field either.'

'Oops!' Greg was grinning as he leaned across and swept his hand over her shoulder. 'I was sure there was a great big chip there but it's gone now, so maybe we can get started. We'll have the first couple in now, Grace.'

Lindy suppressed a shiver at the touch of the long, tapering fingers she remembered so well. Concentrate, girl! she told herself. Stay professional; try to imagine you've only just met this man for the first time. If only!

The dark-haired, thirty-something secretary smiled at Lindy as she went over to the door. Lindy forced herself to smile back as she wondered once more whether she could possibly stand working with this impossible man for three whole months.

As Rona Phillips brought the first couple in she was trying to catch Lindy's eye and mouthing the words 'Why are we in here?' Lindy frowned and gave a slight shake of her head, hoping that Rona wouldn't try to distract her further.

'Chris and Fiona, do come in and make yourselves comfortable,' her boss was saying amiably as he settled his patients in a couple of armchairs which formed a circle with the seats he had already placed. 'I'm Greg Dalton and this is Lindy Cash. I believe you saw Bradley Prestcot last week, but he's asked me to take over because he's tied up in theatre this morning.'

Lindy smiled encouragingly as she watched the large, dark-haired man and his small blonde wife. The husband leaned back against the cushions but his wife sat nervously on the edge of her seat, her fingers clenched so tightly together that the knuckles were white.

'Would you like some coffee?' Greg asked them.

Rona was despatched to get the necessary cups and the breaking of the ice continued. Lindy noticed that Grace was tapping away in her corner, recording nearly every word that was spoken. Chris and Fiona became more and more forthcoming even before they started sipping from their cups. But Lindy noticed that Fiona's cup rattled in the saucer as her trembling hands replaced it.

'Brad tells me you'd like to start a family,' Greg said, making it appear the most natural remark in the world. 'I've got your case notes here but, just remind me, how long have you been married?'

'Ten years,' Chris said. 'Fiona was on the Pill for the first eight; then we decided we could afford to go for a family. Two years we've been trying but nothing's happened.'

Greg leaned back in his chair and gave Chris a sympathetic smile. 'I always think Mother Nature can be so perverse. I mean, there are so many couples who get pregnant when they don't want to, and then there are splendid people like you and Fiona who have to keep on and on trying. Still, it's a good thing the actual method we use to get pregnant is fun, isn't it?'

Chris laughed. 'You can say that again! We've never had any problems in practising.'

Greg gave his patient a rakish grin. 'Well, just remember, Chris, practice makes perfect. Make sure you enjoy yourselves in the process of becoming parents. Once you actually achieve the pitter-patter of tiny feet you won't have as much time to indulge yourselves. Now, fill me in on what's been happening so far.'

The details of the case began to emerge as the husband warmed to his subject. The wife, Lindy noticed, didn't try to interrupt but simply sat, stony-faced, staring straight ahead.

'And we're both thirty-seven, so time's running out,' Chris finished off. 'For Fiona at any rate,' he added, with a faint smile.

Lindy thought that that was a rather insensitive remark. Poor Fiona was looking petrified enough as it was.

'Plenty of time,' Lindy said soothingly, but the wife registered no relief at this pronouncement.

'We started you on some tests last week, didn't we?' Greg said. 'Well, I've got the result of your sperm test here, Chris.'

Greg leaned back across the desk and picked up the path-lab report, his eyes rapidly scanning over it.

He smiled. 'Absolutely nothing to worry about here. Everything normal in terms of semen volume, sperm numbers, sperm mobility and so on. Yes, the little blighters are swimming around happily, and are definitely raring to go. I won't bore you with the technical details unless you want me to.'

Chris was grinning from ear to ear as he shook his head. 'No thanks, Doc. It's such a relief to know there's nothing wrong with me. Not that I ever thought there was, mind you.'

Lindy watched him as he turned to speak to his wife. He looked like a cat who'd licked all the cream from the saucer. 'Like I thought, it must be you.'

'Not necessarily,' Lindy said quickly. She'd had time to scan Fiona's notes as she listened. 'Today we're going to test the hormone level in Fiona's blood to see if she's ovulating normally—in other words, producing eggs for fertilisation. The hormone progesterone is produced by the ovary, which is the place where the eggs are made. Today is the twenty-first day of Fiona's menstrual cycle so if we find a high hormone level in her blood sample this will indicate she's fertile. The high level usually drops off before a period is due and—'

Lindy stopped in mid-sentence and leaped to her feet, striding across the room to catch Fiona before she slumped off the armchair. Her patient's eyes were closed, her skin damp and pallid. Greg was at her side in seconds, lifting the semi-conscious woman onto the examination couch.

'It's nothing to worry about,' Chris said in a bland tone. 'Fiona hates blood tests—in fact, any kind of test. She didn't want to start this treatment in the first place.'

Fiona was opening her eyes, staring up at Lindy with a beseeching look. 'I'm OK, Doctor, really I am. Just felt a bit faint, that's all. Look, could I have a word with you—in private?'

Lindy noticed the way that she was glancing round the room, first at her intimidating husband, then at the expensively suited specialist who, for all his friendly approach, was still a man. And Lindy surmised also that Grace, tapping away in the corner, wasn't helping matters either.

'Come to my room across the corridor and we'll have a chat. No, that's OK, Grace,' Lindy said as she saw the efficient secretary getting up from her chair. 'You stay here and help Dr Dalton.'

Lindy put an arm round her patient's waist to steady her across the corridor, but Fiona seemed to have made a remarkable recovery. Lindy settled her in a chair beside her.

'So what's the real problem, Fiona?' Lindy asked gently.

Her patient burst into tears.

Lindy waited. This often happened, and she'd found

that patients were happier if she didn't fuss. She held a box of tissues in front of Fiona.

'It's all my fault. I. . .'

The distraught patient leaned forward and lowered her voice, as if her words might carry across the corridor to the room opposite.

'I'm still on the Pill.'

'You're what?'

Lindy had heard some strange tales from patients but this was one of the weirdest. Here was a woman being tested for infertility and she was still on the Pill!

'But why? I mean, if you want to start a family, surely the first thing—'

'I don't want to start a family. Chris does but I'm too scared.'

Lindy took hold of her patient's hands. They felt cold and clammy. 'What are you scared of, Fiona?'

'If I have a baby Chris will find out that. . .find out that I had an abortion when I was sixteen.'

'Not unless you tell him,' Lindy said quietly. 'We certainly wouldn't.'

Fiona's eyes widened. 'You mean. . .?'

'A patient's previous medical records are confidential. In this hospital, if a patient confides something personal to their obstetrician, it isn't even written down unless it has life-threatening implications. I certainly wouldn't mention this to anyone unless you asked me to.'

'It was so long ago, but yet I can't forget,' Fiona said softly, her voice breaking with emotion. 'It didn't make sense. I was still at school and I was in love for the first time. I really wanted that baby but my mum made me have an abortion. I cried for days after I lost it.'

Lindy swallowed hard and reached for the tissue box. This was all too close to home. She knew exactly how Fiona felt but she had to remain the calm, detached doctor. Her own problems mustn't be allowed to cloud her treatment of this patient.

'And what about the young father? Did he know anything about it?'

'It was Chris. He would have been furious if he'd known I'd gone behind his back. We've been going out together since we were fifteen. I've always loved him but he likes to be the boss. He scares me when he's angry. . . Oh, don't get me wrong, Doctor; he's not violent—never laid a finger on me in his life. It's just that I can't stand it when he loses his temper and shouts at me.'

'So let's get this straight,' Lindy said cautiously as she wondered to herself why it was that some women, herself included, got involved with the most impossible men. At least she'd had the sense to tell her impossible man where to go, whereas this poor, misguided woman was still hanging on in there. Don't make judgements, said the voice of reason inside her head. Stay calm and professional. Fiona loves Chris, so don't disillusion her.

'You became pregnant by Chris at sixteen; you didn't tell him; your mother insisted you had an abortion. Later you married Chris and—'

'And we were very hard up at first,' Fiona interrupted. 'Needed two wages; couldn't afford kids. Two years ago Chris decided we could afford a family. I told him I'd stopped taking the Pill but—'

'Well,' Lindy put in quickly, sensing a further eruption of tears. 'Would you like a family if there was no danger of anyone hearing about what happened when you were sixteen?'

'Of course I would! I love kids. I would have loved that little mite all those years ago.'

Oh, don't! Lindy thought. Stop turning the knife.

'I'm sure you would, Fiona,' she said quietly. 'So

what you've got to do is come off the Pill, and we'll
see if we can arrange a miracle cure for your infertility.'

Lindy's patient wiped a tissue across her damp face,
removing the black rivers of mascara as she smiled. 'It
would seem like a miracle after two years, wouldn't it?'

'And I'd get all the undeserved credit,' Lindy said
lightly. 'It often happens that when a couple start infertility tests they conceive even before we've given them
any treatment. Nature has a wonderful way of going
about things. But you've got to help by going off the
Pill and relaxing. . .and, of course, propositioning your
husband as often as you can.'

Fiona laughed. 'Oh, that's no problem.'

'Good. Go home, have a good time, and I hope to
see you in the obstetrics department later in the year.
But, whatever you do, don't be tempted to tell Chris
the secret you've kept all these years. From what
you've told me and from what I've seen of him I don't
think he would understand.'

'So what did Fiona want to tell you?' Greg asked Lindy
at the end of the morning.

She'd been trying to escape before he caught up with
her in the glass-paned tunnel that joined the annexe
to the hospital.

'It's confidential.'

'But she's my patient. We should make some
record of it.'

'No, we shouldn't. There are times when we have
to keep secrets and this is one of them.'

'Lindy, look at me.' He put his hand on her arm,
forcing her to stop.

She looked up at him, her heart beating rapidly.
With the wintry sun shining through the melting snow
on the glass she could see every line on his face—the
horizontal creases on his forehead that she'd traced

with her fingers on that fateful night, the dark stubble already showing on his chin even though he'd shaved only hours before. There was a faint aroma of that aftershave she remembered. What was the name? For heaven's sake, does it matter? Concentrate, girl.

'If we're to work together, we mustn't have secrets we don't share,' he said firmly.

She caught her breath and then realised that he was still referring to their patient. How could he know about her own secret. . .their secret?

'I don't think you would understand. And I've promised Fiona I would keep it to myself. But I honestly think we've got a chance of a pregnancy here.'

'OK, you can hold out on me if you feel you've no choice.'

'I have no choice,' she told him firmly, while the confusion in her mind grew.

She began walking rapidly away. She'd been talking about the patient but the last sentence applied to their own situation. They'd reached the dining room. She didn't want to have to sit near him at lunch, surrounded by all her colleagues who would wonder why she couldn't relax in the company of her new boss.

'I'm going to skip lunch today, Greg. Got some phone calls to make,' she muttered as she headed towards the residents' quarters.

She hurried past Casualty, along the white-walled corridor, down one of the impressive, twinned, wide stone staircases that converged at the carved bust of Alexander Fleming set back in the wall, and continued down a single flight of steps to the residents' corridor.

She closed the door of her room, ignoring the chaos, and sank down onto her bed.

Of all the rotten twists of fate: to be thrown together with Greg Dalton! And then to have to listen to a patient sobbing about losing her baby.

A year ago last May she'd been horrified when she'd found out that she was pregnant with Greg's baby, but only because since its conception in the March she'd discovered that he was married. If she was honest with herself, she would have been over the moon to be carrying Greg's baby if he'd been free.

Incredible though it now seemed, it had truly been love at first sight. Even now she remembered the ecstatic vibes she'd felt; the sensual excitement she'd experienced when their eyes had met for the first time had been out of this world. She'd felt as if she'd been whisked away on a magic carpet to a faraway place where the real world didn't exist.

Nothing else had mattered except the deep, urgent feelings which she'd been powerless to control. The sheer wonder of their inevitable lovemaking had been something that she couldn't have imagined in her wildest dreams. It had been like no experience she'd ever had before and certainly not since.

She uttered a choking cry. How could he have deceived her like that?

She turned her head into the pillow as the hot, salt tears stung her eyes. If only he'd been honest with her! But if he'd been honest she never would have experienced that wonderful, impossibly heavenly night. And that was why she'd chosen to go on with the pregnancy—to hold on to the magic of that experience.

She'd cherished that dear little growing baby inside her, been prepared to jeopardise her career for him—she'd been sure it was a boy, someone who would look just like Greg. . .

'Stop it!' she said out loud. 'Stop it now! Enough is enough!'

She sat up and realised that she was shaking, just as she'd shaken when the obstetrician had told her that there was nothing more they could do. They'd tried everything they could to prevent her losing the baby, but in the end her body had decreed otherwise.

'You, as a doctor, must realise that miscarriages sometimes happen spontaneously and often for no particular reason,' the calm, professional obstetrician had told her.

'Yes, I do realise this,' she'd said. 'But it doesn't make it any easier.'

And then she'd cried into her pillow, just the way she was doing now.

CHAPTER TWO

LINDY was feeling decidedly apprehensive. She was going to have to face up to a whole morning in theatre assisting Greg. And she knew for a fact that he didn't want her to be there. He'd scheduled their senior registrar, Sara Clarkson, to be his assistant, but she'd phoned in sick—probably with the gastric flu that was doing the rounds.

She scrubbed her hands vigorously, and then held them out in front of her whilst a nurse slotted her inside the sterile gown.

Bradley Prestcot put his head round the door of the scrub room. 'Everything OK, Lindy?'

'Brad! How's Sara?'

The consultant smiled. 'Oh, she'll survive.'

Lindy thought that there was something odd about the way he glanced around the room before whispering, 'She was a bit sick this morning so I made her stay in bed. By the way, you did get your wedding invitation, didn't you?'

Lindy nodded. 'Oh, Brad, I meant to reply a week ago when it arrived. Only three months to go, isn't it? Maybe Sara's got wedding nerves.'

'Could be,' Brad said mysteriously, and then gave her a big wink.

Lindy smiled. So that was it! How lovely. What a fairy-tale ending to their romance, or rather a good beginning to the next stage; Brad and Sara's wedding wouldn't necessarily mean that they lived happily ever after, although from what she'd seen of the couple since Brad moved into Sara's cottage in

November they were the perfect match.

The scrub nurse had gone out of the room, probably sensing that Brad and Lindy wanted to talk.

'Can I take it that double congratulations are in order?' Lindy said. 'The wedding and. . .?'

Brad grinned. 'And another happy event in September.'

'Brad, I'm thrilled! Tell Sara that—'

'Look, why don't you tell her yourself? I've made her take the whole day off and she'll be champing at the bit by lunchtime. Go over and see her this afternoon if you've got time.'

'I might just do that,' Lindy said, tensing as she saw Greg coming through the door.

Brad chatted to him for a short while, apologising for the fact that Sara couldn't be in theatre that morning.

'Lindy's agreed to stand in so you'll be well taken care of,' Brad finished off before disappearing down the corridor.

Greg's eyes narrowed as he turned his attention on Lindy. 'Have you any experience of microsurgery?' he asked evenly, his face a mask of professional competence.

Lindy's apprehension turned into full-scale nervousness. It had been two weeks since Greg had arrived and she still hadn't conquered her nerves. 'I've studied the theoretical side during my infertility course.'

'But your practical experience is nil?'

'I've had a great deal of experience of conventional surgery and—'

'But no microsurgery?'

'None to speak of. . .I mean, no.'

She faced him across the room as he rolled up his sleeves and began to scrub. The nurse returned and began to pamper him.

He's enjoying having two slaves to dance to his every whim, Lindy thought. But this little slave is going to give him a run for his money! He won't wipe his feet on me this morning!

A group of medical students was gathered in the raised seating area at one end of the operating theatre. Lindy glanced across and remembered that it had only been a couple of years since she'd been a medical student, and here she was, supposedly able to assist this specialist.

'Our first patient, Maria Thomson, is thirty-four,' Greg told the students, who scribbled notes into their files. 'Her Fallopian tubes are blocked; the ovaries are producing eggs but they can't get down to be fertilised. So I'm going to do an operation called cornual anastomosis, in which the blocked part of the tube is removed and the remainder is stitched back onto the original opening. Current statistics show that Maria will then have a forty-five to sixty-five per cent chance of conceiving.

'May I have a scalpel, please, Dr Cash?'

Oh, he was being so polite to her this morning, unlike the other day when he'd ticked her off because she'd failed to anticipate his demands in an outpatient session. Later he'd actually apologised to her, saying that he was under a lot of strain. He hadn't elaborated but she'd taken that to mean his marriage was on the rocks. Serve him right!

She was smiling into her mask as she handed over the instrument that would make the first incision. He needn't think that he could start confiding his marriage problems to her, because she wasn't interested.

She watched, fascinated, as he made the first incision.

'So tiny,' she murmured, half to herself.

The surgeon's eyes above the mask caught hers.

'That's the advantage of microsurgery. It takes a bit longer than conventional surgery but most patients recover far quicker. I'm making what we call in the trade a bikini incision.'

Lindy heard the students scribbling.

'That is a very small cut in the skin, which goes across the pubic-hair line. In six months' time you'll hardly notice the scar, and Maria will be able to run along the beach without feeling self-conscious.'

The delicate operation continued. In spite of herself Lindy admired the way that Greg worked steadily through the intricate surgery. Two hours later he asked if she'd like to finish the final sutures in the abdominal skin and she agreed. Her concentration during the operation had successfully removed some of the tension she usually felt when he was around.

Only when they were leaving theatre did the spectre of the past threaten to return.

'Thanks, Lindy,' Greg said, pausing by the door of the ante-room. 'For a novice in microsurgery you did quite well.'

She swallowed her pride. 'Spare me the lavish praise, Greg.'

'What are you doing this afternoon?' she heard him say.

She continued walking away from him as she peeled off her gown. Underneath, the thin cotton dress was stuck to her skin. She needed a shower and a complete change of clothing. She would go back to her room and indulge in the full works.

'Brad's scheduled me for a half day off so I'm afraid I can't help you out.'

She carried on walking along the corridor.

'I'm not talking about work. I thought you might like to come out to see the cottage I'm buying. I think we need to talk—about our relationship.'

'Oh, no!' She swung round to confront him. 'We said all there was to say on the phone a year last June, remember?'

'Correction! You said all you wanted to say, and it didn't make sense.'

'Probably not to you, but it did to me!'

'There you go again, losing your temper. Can't you cool it long enough to have a sensible discussion, Lindy?'

Mentally she counted up to ten before speaking. 'There's nothing to discuss, Greg. I told you on the phone it had been a mistake, and since meeting up with you again I'm more than ever convinced that I was right.'

She hurried back to her room, to strip off her dress and stand under the shower. As the hot water cascaded over her she began to feel more relaxed.

Maybe Greg was right. Perhaps they should talk. Perhaps it would be better to clear the air. He didn't know that she was aware that he was married. When he'd phoned her at her mother's house in the States nineteen months ago, she'd only been home from hospital a couple of hours, still feeling weak and groggy from the anaesthetic. Hearing Greg's voice had been the last straw. She couldn't remember what she'd said to him, apart from telling him never to contact her again, before she'd slammed the phone down.

She stepped out of the shower and towelled herself vigorously before pulling on a pair of jeans and a hand-knitted Aran sweater. It had been made by Josephine, her faithful schoolfriend, who'd helped her to recover her health on her farm in the Lake District when Lindy had flown back from the States a month after her miscarriage.

Staring at her pale face in the mirror, she rubbed

in a tinted foundation cream and whisked some lipstick across her colourless lips.

'What you need is a holiday, my girl,' she told her reflection.

She could easily go back to the States in April, at the end of her year in the house. But the hospital had invested a great deal in her infertility training, and Brad had hinted that if she lived up to her initial promise in this work they would create a special post for her. She would be getting in at the right time and she could work towards eventually being given a consultancy.

If only Greg Dalton hadn't turned up! She certainly needed to talk. . .but not with him!

She picked up the phone and dialled the number of Sara Clarkson's cottage.

'Sara, this is Lindy. How are you? Brad said—'

'Lindy, how nice of you to call. I can imagine what Brad said, so don't tell me! He got himself all steamed up because I was sick this morning. I'm fine now. Did you have to assist Greg?'

'It was good experience for me. Listen, Sara, I'd like to drop in this afternoon to see you about something. I don't want to talk about it on the phone.'

'Come now. I've made vegetable soup—enough to feed an army, and I don't expect you've had lunch. It's the earth mother coming out in me now that I'm in an interesting condition.'

'Congratulations, Sara! I wasn't sure if I was supposed to know about the baby.'

'Everybody will know via the hospital grapevine soon enough. Come along as soon as you can make it, but drive carefully. The road into Cragdale will be treacherous.'

*   *   *

The road out of Moortown had been heavily salted and gritted to combat the early-morning snowfall. The tyres on Lindy's blue Mini coped well until she reached the narrow, unmade track that led down to Sara's cottage on the outskirts of Cragdale. She had difficulty preventing the car from skidding into a silver Renault Espace parked outside Sara's cottage.

'Hannah!' Lindy recognised another of her medical colleagues coming out of the front door, ahead of Sara, swinging a baby-seat as if it were a shopping bag.

'How's the new baby?' Lindy slammed the door of her car and made her way up the slush-covered garden path.

'Jamie's not so new,' the proud mother said, holding up the baby-seat so that Lindy could get a better look. 'He's three months old.'

'Oh, doesn't he look like Simon?' Lindy said.

Hannah smiled, obviously pleased that he should resemble her handsome husband. 'Do you think so?'

'How does Miles like having a baby brother?' Lindy asked.

'He adores him,' Hannah said. 'Must dash. I only popped in to see how Sara was feeling.'

'It's OK,' Sara said, noticing Hannah's guarded look. 'I've told Lindy the good news. We're going to chat some more over lunch. I wish you'd stay, Hannah.'

'Haven't time. Got a million things to do before collecting Miles from school, but thanks anyway. Bye!'

'Wonderful how everything's turned out for Hannah and me,' Sara said, closing the door and ushering Lindy into her cosy cottage. 'But I gather from Brad that you're not too happy with your present situation. I'm glad you've come to see me, because he asked me to talk to you about it, see what the problem is. Let me give you a sherry to warm you up before lunch.'

They sat either side of a roaring log fire, Lindy pulling off her leather boots and stretching out her toes towards the hearth. She had a sip of sherry, and then another one.

'I hadn't realised Brad had noticed something was wrong.'

Sara smiled. 'He's very observant with his staff. Look, I'm absolutely starving so let's have my casserole in front of the fire while we talk. My digestive system is up the creek at the moment. This morning I couldn't face food. I'll bring that small table up to the fire and—'

'No, I'll bring the table,' Lindy said, with a grin, as she leaped to her feet to help her small, blonde-haired friend, who looked far too fragile to be pregnant. 'Mustn't have you carrying things.'

Sara laughed. 'Now don't start behaving like Brad. Obstetricians are calm and collected until they have babies of their own. Look at Hannah; Simon panicked so much at the beginning of her pregnancy that she had to ask Brad to take care of her.'

'But Brad didn't deliver Hannah's baby, did he?'

'Hannah delivered herself! Simon was away at a conference in Scotland; she phoned me to see if Brad was here because her waters had broken. Brad and I drove as quickly as we could down to her house but young Jamie had already arrived. All we had to do was cut the cord.

'Anyway, enough of this baby talk; what's wrong, Lindy? Brad had the feeling there was a clash of personalities between you and Greg Dalton. Is he right? Don't you get on with the new man?'

Sara was spooning out soup from a huge willow-pattern soup tureen. Lindy watched the steam rising up towards the low oak beams of the minuscule living room. She wiggled her toes in the soft lambswool hearth-rug.

Where should she begin, and how much should she tell? Sara had always been helpful, right from the time when Lindy had arrived at the beginning of her year in the house, feeling slightly in awe of her senior registrar. Sara was still very much her senior, but a true friend. And, after all Sara had been through before she and Brad had finally got together, she had to have an enormous amount of experience to draw on.

'Brad's right. I don't get on with Greg.' Lindy swallowed some more soup. 'This soup's delicious.'

'It will do you good. Lots of nourishing vegetables in there.' Sara waited.

Lindy put down her spoon. 'You see, I knew Greg before he came here. We met in London at my student graduation party. It was in March two years ago. Greg gatecrashed; he was never invited, but I didn't know that until. . .until afterwards. And I didn't know he was married.'

Lindy stopped and looked across at Sara, trying to gauge her reaction.

Sara's gaze didn't falter. 'Did that make a difference?'

'By the end of the night it did.'

Lindy paused and took a deep breath. 'We shared a bottle of champagne together. We were like a couple of kids—having a great time, not a care in the world. We had so much to talk about; it was totally irrational, utter madness, and I fell for it. . .and for him. I suppose it's the nearest I've ever come to experiencing love at first sight.'

A log fell out of the fire onto the hearth. Lindy reached forward and picked up the tongs. 'Let me do it, Sara.' She tossed the smouldering wood back onto the fire, glad of the diversion from her emotionally draining story.

'So what happened after that?' Sara asked quietly.

'I invited him back to my room in the medics hostel for coffee. I didn't want the evening to stop. We finished up in bed and it was. . .' Lindy drew in her breath as that wonderful night returned to her memory. 'Well, it was the most exciting night of my life. I know it sounds corny, but I really thought I was in love, that I'd met the man of my dreams. I mean, I'd never in my life thought I would ever go to bed with someone only hours after meeting him. But it wasn't like that at all. As far as I was concerned, this was going to be for ever. . .'

She took another breath to prepare herself for the painful ending to the story. 'We said goodbye in the early hours of the morning. I had to get myself to Heathrow airport to fly to the States for a two-month holiday, staying with my mother and stepfather.'

She paused. This was the bit that hurt the most. 'There was a fellow student on the tube. He asked me how I'd got on with Greg. With my head in the clouds I said we'd got on like a house on fire. And then he dropped his bombshell. He said, "You know, of course, he's married," and—'

'But he's not any more,' Sara interrupted.

Lindy's heart seemed to do a somersault. 'I'm not surprised!' she blurted out to cover her confusion. 'A woman would be mad to stay with a two-timer like Greg!'

'I don't know any details. All I know is that when Brad phoned him to come up here at such short notice he jumped at it. Said he'd absolutely nothing to keep him in London. He asked what the property market was like up here and Brad told him about a cottage on the other side of the village.

'Cragdale seems to be turning into a medical-staff dormitory, what with Hannah down by the river and Brad and me up here. It's so conveniently near

Moortown and yet far enough to get away from it all. Brad took Greg to see the cottage the day he arrived; it's empty, so Greg's going to move in next week as soon as everything's signed and sealed.'

'I see,' Lindy said, trying to get a grip on her churning emotions. She couldn't quell the excitement she felt on hearing that Greg was a free man, but she was trying to convince herself that it didn't make any difference to her now. It was too late. The hurt was too deep. 'Greg asked me this morning if I'd like to go and see his cottage.'

'Did he now?' Sara said in a knowing voice. 'Well, that sounds to me as if he's still holding a candle for you. I mean, don't you think you're being a bit hard on him, Lindy? It happens all the time these days. Marriages break up, people get divorced.'

'But Greg wasn't divorced when we spent that night together. He should have told me; he shouldn't have led me on to believe he was free.'

'Lindy, it was one night of sheer madness; both of you enjoyed it, so what's the harm, if nobody got hurt?'

Lindy bit her lip to stop herself blurting out that somebody did get hurt. Suddenly she knew that she mustn't tell Sara any more of her story. Sara was one month pregnant, and this wasn't the time for her to hear about her miscarriage. It wouldn't do any good to bring up the awful details, talk about that day when she herself had been almost three months pregnant, loving and wanting the baby inside her because it had been conceived in love.

At the time she'd blocked out the fact that he'd deceived her. She'd been in love with a memory; she'd been going to have her baby and make sure that the reality of the situation never caught up with her, because she'd planned never to see Greg again.

She stared into the flickering flames as she wondered

what would have happened if she hadn't gone swimming that day. She remembered the sudden pain as she'd climbed out of the pool and then had wrapped herself in towels as she'd waited for the ambulance. . .

'Lindy, what's the matter?'

Sara had crossed the hearth-rug and was kneeling down beside her. 'There's something you haven't told me, isn't there?'

Lindy realised that her face was damp with tears. Hastily she dabbed at her eyes with a tissue.

'It's nothing, Sara. You're right; I'm overdramatising the situation. It's over. Thanks for listening. I'll be able to work better with Greg now. All I've got to do is be more professional with him in hospital.'

'But what about your personal relationship with him?' Sara asked, standing up and going back to her armchair.

Lindy forced a sad smile. 'That was over a long time ago. I'll never resurrect it.'

'"Never" is a very final word,' Sara said quietly. 'Brad told me he would never marry a medical woman again because of the experience he'd had with his first marriage, but he changed his mind. People change, circumstances change. I'm not suggesting you should have a full-scale romance, but couldn't you just be friends?'

'On the surface, yes,' Lindy said evenly, trying desperately to quell her emotions. 'But underneath—'

'Lindy, you've changed so much in the two weeks since Greg arrived,' Sara interrupted. 'You always appeared so happy-go-lucky. In fact I thought at first that you didn't take things seriously enough. I don't like to see you being so deadly serious about a one-night relationship. Can't you bury the past and start again?'

'I've blotted it out for nearly two years, Sara,' Lindy said softly. 'I put on my carefree act and fooled everybody, but deep down I couldn't fool myself. It was always there.'

'What was there? There's something else you're not telling me, isn't there, Lindy?'

Lindy nodded wordlessly.

'I won't press you. I value your friendship too much. But if you ever want to confide some more in me. . .'

'Thanks for listening, Sara. Look, I don't want to tire you any more. I'm going to take myself off for a walk over the moors, blow the cobwebs away.'

'Do you think you should? The snow will be thicker up there and. . . Well, talk of the devil!'

Lindy followed the direction of Sara's gaze through the window. A distinctive, sleek black car was purring to a halt outside. Her pulses raced as she leaped to her feet.

'I must go, Sara!'

'Stay a few more minutes, Lindy. It won't hurt you two to meet up here on neutral ground.'

Lindy could feel her heart beating rapidly as she saw Greg walking up the path. He was wearing a brown suede jacket, the collar turned up around a white polo-neck sweater; his jeans were tucked into brown leather fell-boots and he looked devastatingly handsome, just as he had done the first time they'd met.

Sara opened the door.

'Hello, Greg. I was just going,' Lindy said evenly. 'Thanks for the lunch, Sara.'

Greg's hand was on her arm. 'Brad told me you would be here. I thought it would be a good place for a talk. Sara can be the referee.'

She suppressed a shiver at the touch of his fingers. 'We've talked already. Sara's given me some good advice, and now I need some fresh air and exercise, so if you don't mind—'

'I don't mind at all,' Greg said, looking down at her with a rakish grin. 'I'll walk with you.'

'Much more sensible than going by yourself. Take the path behind the cottage,' Sara said quickly. 'Some ramblers went over there this morning so they should have trampled the snow down. You can leave your cars here.'

Lindy's pulses were doing a war dance as Greg took hold of her arm and steered her onto the path that led to the back of the cottage. She knew that it wasn't too late to refuse, but Sara was watching from the door and she wanted to appear polite. Underneath she was seething. How dared he hijack her like this?

They went out through the back gate and climbed the path which rose steeply. Greg was now out in front, and Lindy looked back to see Sara watching from the kitchen window. Sara waved, and Lindy forced herself to smile and return the wave. When she turned back she saw that Greg was waiting for her, a wry grin on his face.

'I think our friend is hell-bent on matchmaking, don't you?' he said, his voice mellow and distinctly provocative.

'No chance!' Lindy said heatedly as she tried to convince herself. 'Let's get one thing straight. I've come on this walk with you under protest. Inside hospital I'll be as polite and professional as you like, but on a personal level just don't push your luck, Greg!'

'Phew! You weren't born with red hair for nothing! And flashing green eyes. That was the first thing I noticed about you—the gorgeous eyes.'

'Keep walking, Greg,' she told him testily. 'I don't want any more of your backhanded compliments. I came up here to recharge my batteries, not to listen to you dragging up the past.'

They walked on in silence to the top of the hill. There was a low wooden seat beside a cairn—one of the piles of stones built at strategic points beside the path to show the way over the hill. Lindy watched as Greg put another stone on the cairn before wiping the snow from the seat with a couple of man-size tissues.

'Your seat, milady,' he said with a flourish.

'How kind,' she replied in an exaggerated tone.

She was very much aware of him seated only inches away as she looked out across the beautiful valley. It was a real winter wonderland. Far below she could make out Hannah's cottage by the river, smoke rising from the chimney. Sara's cottage was now hidden from view. She wondered if Sara was on the phone to Brad telling him that there was nothing to worry about; Lindy and Greg were going to patch things up. How wrong she was!

'So what's this all about? Why the permanent cold shoulder?' Greg said quietly.

She turned to look at him and her heart gave an unexpected little jump. For an instant she remembered the first time she'd seen him. It was certainly corny but their eyes had actually met across a crowded room! It was the sort of thing you read about in romantic novels but never believed would happen in real life. But it had happened to them. Otherwise she would never have agreed to going to bed so quickly.

She'd looked across and seen this tall, dark, hand-some stranger, and bingo! Something inside her had said that they were made for each other, that this was going to be the one and only man in her life.

She'd felt as if a hand was squeezing her heart, giving her cardiac massage to stop her from fainting away. The room had actually seemed to spin round, and she hadn't registered the noisy chatter any more. Greg had told her later in bed that he'd felt exactly the same and that was why he'd walked right across the room, pushing his way through the crowd to get to her and say, 'Haven't we met somewhere before?'

She'd laughed at the sheer audacity of the man and told him that it was a good chat-up line, not very original but he could buy her a drink if he liked. He'd bought a bottle of champagne and they'd settled themselves in a corner, oblivious to all that was going on around them.

'Do I get a reply to my question, Lindy, or are you going to keep staring in silence at me? You look as if you've seen a ghost.'

'I feel as if I have,' she said quietly, turning away. 'I was. . .I was remembering.'

He put out his hand and his fingers closed over hers.

'It was good, wasn't it, Lindy?' he said gently.

She didn't dare to move, to face him and look into his eyes. It would be all too poignant for her. The clasp of his hand was unnerving her completely.

'Yes, it was good,' she whispered in a barely audible voice. 'But that was before I found out you were married. Don't you realise how devastated I was after I'd spent the night with you? Why didn't you tell me?'

His voice was gravelly, sexy, suggestive. 'If I'd told you, would you have spent the night with me?'

She gave a harsh laugh. 'What do you take me for? I do have some standards, and one of them is never to try and steal another woman's man.'

'That's very commendable, but not everybody has your standards.' His voice was bitter now. 'Six months before I met you I discovered my wife, Jane, was having an affair with my best friend. Bob had been best man at our wedding. We worked in the same obstetrics department. I had absolutely no idea until

I went home early one day and found the two of them in our bed.'

'Oh, no! What did you do?'

'I was tempted to beat the living daylights out of Bob, but then I reasoned that Jane must have gone willingly to bed. If I couldn't trust her then our relationship was over. I went straight back to hospital, to my room in the residents' quarters. I phoned my solicitor and made an appointment for the next day to start divorce proceedings.'

'You don't let the grass grow under your feet, do you?'

He grunted. 'What's the point? If a relationship is over, it's over. The divorce proceedings got under way and I stayed in the residents' quarters, turning myself into something of a hermit when I was off duty, I suppose. I avoided all the usual social situations and kept myself to myself, licking my wounds and planning never to trust another woman as long as I lived.

'And then, on the night I met you, I remember hearing music coming from the students' hostel across the car park. I saw the bright lights and decided I'd been hibernating too long. It was time to start living again. I decided to start my new freedom by gatecrashing a party—something I hadn't done since student days. I was feeling pretty reckless, I can tell you.'

'And you thought you'd pick up the first available female and carry her off to bed.'

'No!' He seized her by the shoulders, forcing her to turn and face him. 'It wasn't like that! I intended to stay a few minutes, just long enough to break out of my self-imposed shell. And then I saw you. . .'

His voice trailed away. Lindy waited, hardly daring to breathe. His face was oh, so close to hers, and she found herself fighting the magnetic force of his charismatic personality.

'Do you remember, Lindy, how it was when we met?' he said in a sexily husky voice.

Her knees had turned to jelly. She was so glad that she was sitting down. Oh, yes, she remembered! But she'd tried so hard to forget and she mustn't weaken now, even though. . .

He was pulling her towards him and she didn't resist. When his sensual lips claimed hers she closed her eyes, savouring the moment as she had done on that fateful night. And, just as had happened two years ago, the touch of his lips sent a frisson of raw passion tingling down her spine, awakening all the dormant sensuality locked away inside her.

His hands moved to caress her, and she felt her breasts straining against the constraints of her bra, longing for the arousing touch of his sensitive fingers. Her mind blocked out the past; the present was a fairy tale in which she was being wooed once more by her Prince Charming.

She heard herself give a low moan of release as his fingers found their way inside her jumper, unhooked her bra and began to explore her skin, sending shivers of ecstasy shooting over her body, down her spine, igniting the fires deep down inside her. She could feel his hard body moulding his virile manhood against her soft, compliant feminine curves. She was losing control of herself, and, just as before, she neither wanted nor felt capable of resisting.

But as his caressing hands moved lower, reaching the starved parts of her body that were aching to open up to him, some tiny semblance of common sense reared its head and told her to hold back. She mustn't go on; she must stop before she was hurt again.

As she tensed and made a movement of resistance she felt Greg pull himself away.

'Don't slap my face,' he said quietly. 'I just had to

do that for old times' sake. You made it perfectly clear that time when I phoned you that we'd made a one-off mistake. I must admit that I could have wished you'd wrapped it up a bit instead of screaming at me in that demented way. But since I've met up with you again and had to endure your temper tantrums I've realised that's what I must expect from you!'

His words were like a bucket of cold water over her head! She was back to reality with a vengeance.

'Temper tantrums! What about you? Always criticising me, finding fault, trying to undermine my confidence. No wonder I have to blow my top occasionally!'

She scraped back her red hair from her forehead and glared at him to counteract the frustration she felt as she tried to dispel the sensuous waves still running over her. He'd been quite right when he'd said that he shouldn't have done that! It was too evocative by far. What did he think she was made of—ice? But ice would melt, in just the way that she was trying not to do now.

He dropped his hands from her shoulders and moved to the other end of the seat. All at once she noticed that it was a very cold day.

'As I see it, we've got to have a pact if we're to work together,' he said. 'We can't jeopardise the smooth running of the infertility clinic and the obstetrics department just because we have a private axe to grind. I'll be totally civil if you will. That's all I wanted to say to you this afternoon and I've had to chase you to the top of a mountain to get an audience. I don't know why you couldn't have come over to my cottage. You can just see it at the other side of the valley over there.'

He leaned across so that he could point it out. 'See the narrow, twisting road between the high walls leaving the village? Follow it to the second bend and there on the left. . .'

'The pink house?' she asked, screwing up her eyes as an unexpected shaft of sun appeared through the glowering snow clouds.

He laughed. 'Yes. Isn't it a ghastly colour? I'm going to paint it white.'

'I think it looks rather pretty. I like pink. And it stands out so beautifully in the snow, don't you think?'

Their eyes met again. She held her breath. 'I didn't come to see it today because. . .'

He was smiling in a decidedly seductive way. 'Because you thought I would proposition you, didn't you? Maybe try to pick up where we left off?'

She nodded. 'Something like that.'

There was an enigmatic smile on his face as he stood up. 'I got a bit carried away just now; it's so easy to get roused when you're close to someone you've spent the night with. But, I assure you, when I invited you out to the house today nothing was further from my mind.'

'Well, that's a relief,' she said, trying to rally her plummeting spirits.

CHAPTER THREE

LINDY was enjoying working for the whole morning on Nightingale. It was good to get away from the tension she felt when she was working with Greg in the infertility unit. For the last couple of weeks their professional politeness pact had held but it had been a strain. Sometimes she wondered how much longer she could keep it up, because it wasn't just the effort of being civil to the man who'd disrupted her life, it was all the other niggling sensations she had when she was near him.

He was, without doubt, a dangerously charismatic man, and she could see why she'd previously fallen for him like that. What was more unnerving was the feeling that if she didn't keep a tight rein on her emotions she could so easily go down the same path again, and she was determined not to do that. Greg was part and parcel of the awful emotional upheaval that had changed her life for the worse, and as long as he was around she couldn't begin to forget.

She leaned over one of the cots in the prem unit, checking the pulse and respiration of the tiny scrap inside. She watched the flickering heartbeat on the monitor. So far so good with this little one, she thought, but there was a long way to go.

'Young Samantha is holding her own, Dr Cash,' said Sister Gregson, bustling over from her desk in a swish of starch.

Ann Gregson was one of the old school who had declined to wear the newer uniform which didn't

43

require an apron or cap. Now in her fifties, and having run Nightingale for the past fifteen years, she disliked change and thought that her nurses, in their more casual uniform, weren't half as smart now as they had been in her day.

'I'm not too happy about her colour,' Lindy said. 'Have we got the results of her blood test?'

'Just arrived. The bilirubin level is too high.'

Lindy nodded her head as she studied the path-lab report that Sister had given her.

'It appears to be a physiological jaundice which, as we both know, is due to the normal breakdown of red blood cells that occurs after birth. Samantha was premature and, as so often occurs in prems, the rate of breakdown is greater than the rate of elimination of bile pigments from the bloodstream. Three days old; this is a fairly typical time for it to happen. Is the mother breast-feeding, Sister?'

'I'm afraid not. She was very weak after the birth; she tried but couldn't manage.'

'Well, try giving Samantha some extra fluids; sterile water should improve her condition, and we'll give her some phototherapy by putting her under our special blue lamp for a few hours each day. The blue spectrum of light will help in converting the fat-soluble bilirubin to water-soluble bilirubin which will pass out in the baby's stools. You'll have to be very careful about watching her temperature and making sure her skin doesn't get too dry.'

'Of course,' Sister Gregson said.

'I'll set it up before I do the rest of my round.'

'Dr Dewhirst will bring the equipment for you and give you a hand,' Sister said, hurrying over to speak to their junior registrar.

'Thanks, James,' Lindy said as her tall, brown-haired colleague returned with the lamp. 'Sister Gregson likes to make use of her male staff. I could perfectly well have set it up myself.'

James Dewhirst grinned. 'Well, it's good to have an excuse to work with you again, Lindy. We don't see nearly enough of you these days. How's the work going over in the infertility clinic?'

'The work's fine. I love it. I'm thinking of specialising in infertility. . .but maybe not in this hospital.'

'Why ever not? You've got it made here! It'll be a lot harder to be accepted somewhere else. Besides, I thought you and. . .'

Lindy turned baby Samantha onto her back and carefully fixed tiny dark goggles over her eyes.

'There you are, my lovely,' she cooed. 'We'll soon have you looking even more beautiful. You can switch on the lamp now, James. That's good.'

She straightened up and turned to look at her colleague. 'What was that you were saying? You thought there was some reason why—'

'Oh, come on, Lindy. It's all round the hospital about you and Greg. You knew each other before, didn't you?'

'Briefly,' she replied quietly, looking back at her tiny patient. 'Tell me, what have you heard on the grapevine?'

James Dewhirst glanced across at the nursing station but Sister Gregson had disappeared into her office. He lowered his voice.

'Everybody's waiting to see when you're going to start going out together again. The general consensus is that it's only a matter of time. Is that true?'

'Is what true?' said a deep male voice.

Lindy, who was facing the door, had seen Greg walking down through the cots while James had been speaking. She'd been trying to signal to the young registrar to be quiet but he hadn't cottoned on quickly enough.

'Come on, James; what, or rather who, were you talking about?' Greg asked, a wry smile on his face.

James was looking decidedly embarrassed. 'I was only repeating what everyone is speculating about— whether you and Lindy are going to get together.'

Greg gave Lindy an extremely seductive smile. 'Who knows? I'd like to see you at the end of the morning, Lindy. I'm actually looking for Sister. She's got an IVF patient of mine from London in here, and I want to check how near we are to delivery.'

He was already halfway down the ward but turned back to call, 'Twelve o'clock in my consulting room, Dr Cash.'

Lindy saw the rakish grin on Greg's face. He was up to something! There was no need to let the whole ward know that they were meeting, even though it would be on a perfectly professional footing.

She tried to ignore the meaningful glances that passed between Beryl Frost and Jean Smith, two of the staff midwives, who were making up an admission bed a few feet away as she went into one of the side-wards to check on Samantha's mother.

Her work throughout the morning required her full concentration, but in between patients she couldn't help thinking about the way that Greg had behaved towards her this morning. Politeness was one thing, but being downright provocative in front of other colleagues just wasn't on!

At the end of the morning she confronted Greg the moment she walked into his room.

'What do you think you're playing at, Greg?'

'Careful, Lindy, your professional mask is slipping. Do sit down.'

He motioned towards a chair but remained at the other side of the desk, continuing to sign his name on the pile of letters in front of him.

'James Dewhirst had just told us that the grapevine is buzzing with false accounts of a fictitious affair between us and you go and invite me to your room in front of the whole of Nightingale! How do you think I felt?'

He smiled as he put down his pen and pushed the letters to the back of the desk. 'I've no idea how you felt. You'll have to tell me.'

His deep brown eyes were relentlessly scrutinising her face, and suddenly she ran out of steam. She'd been spoiling for a fight all morning but those calm, expressive, infinitely sensuous eyes had taken the wind out of her sails.

'Well, I felt embarrassed,' she finished lamely.

He stood up and came round to her side of the desk. 'Well, you'll just have to get rid of the embarrassment if you want to hold onto your job.'

She frowned. 'What on earth are you talking about?'

'Let me explain.' He pulled a chair nearer to her and sat down. 'Brad has asked me to speak to you about our relationship. No, let me finish, Lindy,' he said emphatically as she tried to butt in. 'Reports have filtered back to him that you've been over-familiar to the point of rudeness with me when we've been working together.

'Now, as you know, Brad has a vested interest in this clinic. His father's company put up the money to get us started, and he's promised to make a success of it. The clinic will run smoothly if we have a male and a female doctor working harmoniously together, not a couple continuously finding fault with each other.'

'You're as much to blame as I am, Greg,' Lindy put in heatedly.

'I know. So we have two choices.'

She stared at him. 'What are you leading up to?'

'Brad has told me that they're going to create a special position here for a junior female doctor to assist me. He'd very much like to give the post to you when you finish your year in the house in April—but only if you can control your temper and stop snapping at me in an over-familiar way.'

Lindy drew in her breath. How dared they discuss her behind her back! This was the last straw! She would tell them what they could do with their special job.

'As far as I'm concerned—' she began angrily, but Greg wouldn't let her finish.

'Hang on a minute! Let me finish before you make a decision, Lindy,' he said firmly.

'This is the job of a lifetime for a young junior doctor. You wouldn't get a position like this outside this hospital. Oh, no! You're in the right place at the right time, so don't turn it down out of pique.'

Lindy swallowed, hard. Greg was right. It was a golden opportunity. She'd be a fool not to take it. 'You said there were two choices. What's the other one?'

'Brad will advertise the post and select another female doctor to assist me. I can tell you he's already had numerous enquiries about the post. Now, I don't mind who assists me. It's up to you.'

Again she swallowed; a feeling of despondency ran over her as she heard Greg saying that he didn't mind who assisted him. Didn't she count for anything any more? His cool, analytical approach was in direct contrast to the way he'd behaved on Nightingale earlier.

She frowned. 'But what has all this got to do with your weirdly suggestive manner on the ward this morning?' she asked slowly.

'I'll tell you, but only if you've decided to let it be known that you want to stay on. What's it to be?'

Her job was beginning to appeal even more, but she didn't want to think why. And curiosity about what Greg was up to was getting the better of her. If he made advances again would she be able to resist him? And what was *more* galling to her was wondering whether she wanted to resist. Looking at him now, sitting so close to her. . .

She nodded. 'You're right about the job. I'd be a fool not to continue working here.'

'Good girl! Well, here's what I've figured out. You and I know there's nothing going on between us, but the rest of the staff are dying for another romance. They've had two successes recently. Hannah married Simon, Brad's going to marry Sara. They're in the doldrums and they want another romance to focus on. Why don't we let them think we're going to be the next in line for wedding bells?'

'Why should we?'

'Because that way, whenever our professional mask slips—as it's sure to, especially where you're concerned. I mean look at the way you burst in here this morning— No, let me finish. That way they'll just think we've had a lover's tiff and we won't be accused of unprofessional behaviour. I'm as keen on climbing the career ladder as you are, but if word gets around that we're difficult to work with we're neither of us going to get very far.'

Lindy frowned. 'I'm not sure if—'

'Look, the point is we both find it a strain working together, and half the time we're putting on an act trying to be polite for the sake of our careers. The grapevine is convinced we've got something going between us. We don't have to do anything about it. Just don't deny any rumours; keep everybody guessing and they'll forgive us any time we start criticising each other.'

He moved swiftly and she felt his arms pulling her against him. She gasped as his mouth swooped down on hers. She was facing the door and she saw it opening. Grace, coming in to collect the signed letters, was standing in the doorway, her eyes showing how startled she was. Hurriedly she closed the door again.

'Greg, you beast!' Lindy pulled herself away, but not before the tingling feeling on her lips had begun to spread over her entire body. 'You knew Grace would be coming in for the letters. You did that on purpose!'

He gave a boyish laugh. 'I won't do it again, I promise, Lindy! I just wanted to add some fuel to the fire.'

Greg's phone was ringing. He swung round to the desk. 'Yes, Sister Gregson?'

As Lindy watched him she felt a pang of confused emotion running through her. She didn't like the way he'd spelled out their relationship, pointing out that there was nothing going on between them, promising never to kiss her again, never to hold her in his arms. Was that what she wanted? She'd thought it was, until he'd walked back into her life.

'Of course I'm coming,' she heard Greg say. 'I promised my patient I'd be with her when she was delivered. That's why she's come all the way from London.'

He was smiling as he leapt to his feet.

'My IVF patient has gone into labour. I've got to go.'

She surprised herself by saying, 'May I come with you? I've never delivered a patient who's had in vitro fertilisation.'

'Good experience for you. Yes, come along by all

means, although, as you know, it's no different from a normal birth.'

He ushered her out through the door.

She noticed that his hand was under her arm as he steered her through the outer office where his secretary kept her eyes firmly fixed on her computer. The show of pseudo-affection had started, she told herself, so how would she be able to distinguish between the real thing and the put-on-for-effect?

He outlined his patient's case history as they hurried along the corridor through to the main hospital, and up the stairs to Nightingale.

'Jill Barton is in her mid-thirties,' he told her. 'We discovered her ovaries weren't ovulating normally. We put her on fertility drugs; the ovaries produced eggs but still she didn't conceive. So we removed some of her eggs and selected the best ones for fertilisation with her husband's sperm, after which we transferred the most viable embryos inside her uterus. One of them has gone to full term.

'She's thrilled at the prospect of the baby, as you can imagine, but she wanted me to be there at the delivery, probably because I've been in charge of the whole operation right from the start of her treatment. Her husband brought her up here a couple of days ago.'

'And all this so that you could deliver her?' Lindy said. They were walking through the doors of the delivery room.

'Some people do actually appreciate my medical skills,' he said under his breath. 'Can't think why you've found me so difficult to work with.'

She stemmed the retort that sprang to her lips. She'd got to keep her cool!

The patient was being wheeled in. Greg went across to speak to her.

'Jill, how are you doing?'

'Thank goodness you're here, Dr Dalton. My husband's had to go back to London—some crisis in the office; he doesn't know I've gone into labour. How long will it take?'

'Good question, Jill,' Greg replied calmly. He was checking the monitor. 'Shouldn't be too long. Good, strong contractions coming now. Breathe into this mask when you feel one coming. I'm going to scrub up and then I'll be with you all the time.'

Lindy followed Greg out to the scrub room. A nurse fixed them into their gowns.

'It's a good feeling to be delivering a baby in what seemed like a hopeless case,' he said as they walked back into the delivery room.

He examined the birth canal. 'Dilating rapidly now,' he told Lindy. 'Hold Jill's hand and make sure she pants. I don't want a tear in the perineum.'

The patient clung onto Lindy's hand. Lindy took a piece of gauze and wiped Jill's face.

'Thanks, Doctor. Will it be long. . .? Ooh. . .'

'Pant, Jill,' Lindy said urgently.

'I've got the head,' Greg said. 'Keep panting, Jill.'

There was a pause between contractions. Jill lay back against the pillows. Lindy squeezed her hand. 'You're doing extremely well. We're nearly there.'

She could see Greg checking that the umbilical cord wasn't round the baby's neck. He nodded to Lindy that all was well.

When the next contraction came Lindy told Jill to push hard. The shoulders appeared and then the tiny body slipped out.

The new mother smiled as she heard a thin, wailing cry.

'You've got a beautiful daughter, Jill,' Greg said,

handing over the baby, which he'd wrapped in a dressing towel.

'Oh, she's gorgeous!' Jill said. 'Just wait till Alan sees her! It's like a miracle. I never believed—'

She broke off and turned to Lindy. 'Have you got children, Doctor?'

Lindy swallowed hard. The pain was never far below the surface. 'No, but I can imagine how. . .' She stopped in mid-sentence as her eyes met Greg's.

There was an enigmatic expression on his face as he pulled off his sterile gloves. 'Take over here, Sister,' he said quietly. 'All the usual checks, please. I'll be back in a few minutes.'

He was coming towards her. Lindy stood up, feeling her legs shaking. It had been a mistake to be in on a birth with Greg. It was all too poignant for her. She would have had to be made of stone not to be moved by it. But she had to continue working with him and there would be other occasions when they would deliver babies together.

She'd reached the swing-doors before he caught up with her.

'Are you all right, Lindy?' His voice was concerned.

He put his arm around her as they went out together. Was this another show for their watching colleagues? The feel of his fingers on her waist made her tremble. They were standing in the scrub room now. The scrub nurse took one look at them and went out.

'I'm OK,' Lindy said in a shaky voice, raising her eyes to his.

Gently he cupped her face with his fingers. 'You don't look OK. What's the matter, Lindy?'

She put her hands to her face, intending to remove his tantalising fingers. The last thing she needed was his sympathy. But as her hands covered his she felt a tremor of emotion running through her. Reluctantly she pulled his hands away.

'There's no need to overdo the romantic charade, Greg,' she said unsteadily. 'There's no one watching us so you don't have to appear concerned about me. I'm overtired, that's all.'

'That's not all! You're keeping something back. What is it, Lindy?'

His arms were round her now, tightening in an unnerving embrace that brought back too vivid memories.

She looked up into his expressive eyes and shivered as her treacherous body threatened to melt against him just as it had on that fateful night, but she knew that that would only reopen the wounds that she was trying to heal. With a tremendous effort she pulled herself away.

'I can't tell you, Greg.'

She began to walk away and this time he let her go. She reached her room and sank down on the bed, telling herself that she must never tell Greg about the baby she'd lost. And neither must she read anything into the tender concern he'd shown for her tonight. It was all part of the romantic play-acting, nothing more. . .

This was the easiest way of dealing with their complicated relationship. . .wasn't it?

CHAPTER FOUR

'I THINK it's so romantic,' Staff Nurse Rona Phillips said wistfully as she leaned over Lindy's chair to place a pile of case notes on her desk. 'When Sara marries Brad on the Saturday before Easter that will be our second wedding in a year. Hannah and Simon got married last April, didn't they? Now, I wonder who'll be next?'

'I wonder,' Lindy said in an expressionless voice.

In the last couple of months, since Greg had come up with the idea of inventing a romantic liaison between them, she'd become more than a little tired of the innuendoes directed towards her.

The door flew open. 'I need a word in private, Lindy,' Greg said smoothly.

'I was just on my way out, Dr Dalton,' Rona said, with a knowing look at Lindy. She called back as she left, 'I'll come back later.'

'Greg, do you have to do that?' Lindy asked testily, swivelling round in her chair.

'Do what?' He was grinning from ear to ear.

'You know very well. Couldn't you say what you have to say in front of Rona?'

The smile vanished and Greg became deadly serious. 'No, I couldn't, because it concerns our patients, Fiona and Chris Baxter. They're coming in this morning. The last time they were here, in January, we saw them together before Fiona had a private consultation with you, after which you refused to tell me what she said.'

'Ah! Yes, I see what you mean,' she hedged, playing for time.

55

'So, as I see it, I can't go ahead until I know the full facts of the case.'

Lindy cleared her throat nervously as she remembered how their patient Fiona had been deceiving her husband into thinking she'd stopped taking the Pill. She knew that she was treading a tightrope by concealing this and the secret of Fiona's teenage pregnancy, but she'd made a solemn promise to her and she couldn't break it.

'Trust me, Greg. I'll tell you the facts, but not yet.'

'You really are the most obstinate colleague I've ever worked with,' he said, frowning deeply as he sank down into the patient's chair beside Lindy's desk. 'I'm supposed to be in charge of this infertility unit. It's rank insubordination, but I'll forgive you this time if you'll have dinner with me tomorrow night. It's a boring board of governors function and I have to take a lady; so, as we're supposed to be romantically linked, I thought you would be ideal, just as long as you can be civil to me all evening.'

'I don't think I could,' Lindy said.

'Could what? Come to the bun-fight, or remain civil all evening?'

'Both. Look, Greg, I'm getting tired of this silly charade. I'm sick of people asking how we're getting on together when there's absolutely nothing going on at all.'

'Then let's remedy that,' he said, leaning towards her with a rakish grin.

His arms were reaching out for her. She pushed her chair back, well aware that his embrace would only be an act, but knowing that any physical contact with Greg was unnerving to say the least.

He laughed. 'Sometimes I think you're petrified of me, and I wonder what I ever did to deserve the way you treat me.'

She shivered involuntarily. 'Greg, be serious for a moment. This pseudo-affair really is getting out of hand.'

'I don't have any problem with it. When people ask questions I simply give them a mysterious smile and suggest they mind their own business. I don't deny the rumours, but I don't do anything to make people think they're true. The only drawback for me is that while I'm supposed to be linked with you I can't take anyone else out. Which is basically why I'm stuck with you for the governors' banquet.'

'Thanks very much! That's very noble of you. But don't forget it works the same way for me. My nights on the town have been few and far between recently,' she flung at him. 'So maybe we should put the record straight, cancel the non-existent affair.'

'Only if you can be totally professional and behave like the rest of the staff,' Greg said in a serious tone. 'Your job's on the line if Brad gets reports about you being unprofessional and difficult to work with.'

'It's so much easier for you,' Lindy burst out in frustration. 'You haven't been through—'

She stopped in mid-sentence, aware that she'd been going to say too much.

His expressive eyes were searching her face. 'Been through what, Lindy?'

Been to hell and back, she thought, but she knew that she couldn't tell him about the miscarriage or the terrible guilt that haunted her when she remembered how the obstetrician in the States had advised her not to swim for the first three months. She'd been pregnant for almost three months that warm summer day, and she'd felt so well, so bubbling with vitality. She'd been convinced that she wouldn't harm the baby, convinced that her obstetrician was being over-cautious.

Alex Grainger had been recommended to her by her

stepsister, Lucy, who was a nurse in the local hospital. Lindy had confided in Lucy after doing her own pregnancy test at six weeks. She'd been in a state of shock and hadn't been able to decide what to do. One thing she hadn't wanted to do at that stage had been to confide in her mother or her stepfather, but she got on well with Lucy, who'd been very supportive.

After the initial shock, during which she'd actually considered the possibility of a termination, she'd begun to remember the wonderful night when her baby had been conceived and the love she'd felt for Greg before she'd known that he was married. And so she'd wanted that love-child more than anything else in the world.

She gave an involuntary sigh.

'Lindy? What's the matter? *What* have you been through?' he repeated in a gentle voice.

She realised that she'd been staring into space, a strained expression on her face.

'Women colleagues tend to ask me more questions than they would dare with you,' she improvised quickly. 'It's like a never-ending inquisition.'

'Why do I always have the distinct impression you're keeping something from me?'

She gave a harsh laugh. 'I can't answer that.'

He leaned across and took hold of her hands. For a few moments she allowed herself to relax. The sensation of his fingers clasping hers was evoking memories. She was tempted to admit that it wasn't Greg's fault that everything had gone so terribly wrong. If only she could remember the beginning of their relationship and not the horrible ending of it.

'About our patients, Chris and Fiona,' he said briskly, leaning back and clasping his hands in front of him.

'May I suggest that Fiona comes in here to see me by herself and you talk to Chris?' Lindy said quickly, relieved that she could concentrate on a professional matter.

Again Greg frowned. Lindy couldn't do anything to stop the way her emotions churned when she looked at him now. The misshapen nose seemed to enhance his ruggedly handsome face. The aura of virility that surrounded his huge frame was intensely disturbing to her. How had she come to be mixed up with a man like this? A man who irritated her so much that she couldn't bear him, but whom, when he came near her, she wanted to stay even though she was too proud to admit it.

'OK, we'll play it your way,' Greg said in a grudging voice. 'But I hope you're being totally professional with Fiona, and I hope you know what you're doing. Brad tells me your contract as a junior house surgeon expires next week, so you'll be totally reliant on getting another contract for this specially created post in the infertility unit. Don't blot your copybook, my girl.'

'I won't. . .and I'm not your girl.'

'Heaven forbid!' he replied, hauling himself to his feet. 'And heaven help any poor man who tries to tame you. I'd rather get a job in a lion's cage.'

He bent his head so that his face was oh, so close to hers. She shivered as his hot breath fanned her face but she remained rooted to the spot, mesmerised by those dark, expressive eyes. He grasped her by the shoulders, his eyes searching her face.

'If only I knew what was going on in that pretty little head,' he murmured, half to himself, before his lips swooped down on hers.

For a moment she struggled before giving in to the delicious sensation of desire running through her. His sensuous lips sent shivers of passion shooting through her body. How long she remained in his arms she didn't know, but when he pulled away she felt bereft of all emotion except longing—longing for what might have been, longing for what still might be.

'Were you hoping that Rona would come in and see us?' Lindy asked, to cover the embarrassment she felt at her wholehearted participation.

He gave her a teasing grin. 'What makes you think that wasn't for real? You're certainly a good actress yourself. If I hadn't known that you dislike me so much I would have said that— Ah, Rona, just in time,' he finished off smoothly, with a smile at the returning staff nurse. 'You'd better come into my consulting room when Fiona and Chris arrive. Lindy wants a private consultation with Fiona in here.'

Rona smiled. 'No problem, sir.'

Greg paused at the door. 'So was that a yes or a no, Lindy?'

'Sorry?'

'The governors' banquet tomorrow night. On or off?'

Talk about putting her on the spot! she thought furiously. 'I'll check my diary.'

'I need to know by this afternoon; if you can't make it I'll have to find a replacement.'

She felt like throwing something at the closing door!

'Wow! I wouldn't need to check my diary,' Rona said.

Lindy didn't need to check hers! As she'd told him, she'd had precious little social life in the last couple of months. Why not go out to celebrate the end of her year in the house and, hopefully, the beginning of her career as an infertility expert? It wouldn't do her career any harm at all to be seen with Dr Greg Dalton who was carving out a niche for himself as a specialist in the subject. She would take the evening in a light-hearted way, try to imagine that she'd never met Greg before.

'Would you like to bring in the first patients, Rona?'
Lindy said briskly.

She gave all her attention to the first two couples
who came in. Both were first appointments so she
scheduled the necessary tests for both of them and
arranged for further appointments. The next couple
were Fiona and Chris Baxter. Rona brought Fiona in
before going over to Greg's consulting room
with Chris.

Lindy smiled at her patient. 'Nice to see you
again, Fiona. Sit down and tell me how things are
going.'

'I gave up the Pill like you said, Doctor, and,
well. . .I think. . .in fact I'm sure I'm. . .'

Lindy looked at her patient's happy face. 'You think
you're pregnant?'

Fiona nodded. 'Chris couldn't understand how keen
I was in bed. I think I wore him out sometimes. I've
never been so. . . Well, anyway, I bought one of those
pregnancy-test kits from the chemist, and it's positive.
I haven't told Chris yet. I thought I'd get confirmation
from you first and then we'll have to concoct a story
so he doesn't know I was still on the Pill until two
months ago. What shall I say?'

'Say nothing,' Lindy said quickly. 'It sometimes happens, when a couple come to the infertility unit. If
there's nothing clinically wrong with them, the fact that
something is being done about the problem seems to
trigger Mother Nature into action. If Chris asks questions we'll say that's what it must be.'

'He'll be over the moon! It's been so hard to keep
it from him since I did the test last week.'

'Well, let's check it out first,' Lindy said, reaching
for Fiona's urine-sample bottle. 'There is just one thing
I need to clear up. I'd like to be able to confide the
truth to Dr Dalton. It will go no further and I certainly

won't write anything down, but he is my boss and it would be difficult to keep it from him much longer.'

'As long as it's only Dr Dalton I don't mind. I think he's gorgeous. Yes, let him in on the secret. He has a right to know.'

'He has a right to know.' The words lingered in Lindy's mind as she took some blood from her patient before picking up the phone and requesting someone to collect the samples for clinical testing.

And as she began her examination of Fiona the words kept coming back to her. Yes, Greg had a right to know his patient's secret. But what about her own secret? The fact that she'd denied him fatherhood by ignoring her obstetrician's advice, thinking that she could take care of herself and her unborn child—Greg's unborn child. With a determined effort she gave all her attention to her patient and banished the thoughts of her own problems.

Fiona was thrilled when Lindy pointed out the flashing heartbeat of the tiny foetus on the ultrasound screen. All the indications were that the pregnancy was about six weeks on.

'This is the earliest we can be sure of seeing the heartbeat on the screen,' Lindy explained. 'And the date of your last period ties in with this too. When we get the results of your blood tests back we'll be able to see if your hormone level is what it should be at six weeks.'

At the end of the examination Lindy asked her to get dressed again.

'We'll go across to see your husband and tell him the good news when you're ready, Fiona.'

The patient drew in her breath. 'I'm so nervous. I know he'll be thrilled, but you don't think he'll guess I've only just come off the Pill, do you, Doctor?'

'Only if you tell him.'

'Which I won't! And the abortion?'

'All in the past,' Lindy replied firmly, wishing that she could say the same about her own problems. 'Come on, let's go across the corridor and break the good news.'

The look that passed between Greg and Chris when Lindy announced that Fiona was pregnant was one of pure amazement.

Greg appeared to recover his professional cool quickly. 'It sometimes happens when couples seek infertility treatment that they conceive before the actual treatment has started.'

Lindy flashed him a grateful smile. He couldn't have said anything better if she'd primed him!

'Fiona. . .darling. . .' Chris was staggering to his feet, crossing the room to gather his wife into his arms. 'You clever old thing.'

'Hey, not so much of the "old" if you don't mind,' Fiona said laughingly. 'I'm only thirty-seven, like you.'

'I must admit I've felt ancient during the last couple of months,' Chris said, hugging his wife against him. He turned to look at Greg and Lindy, a contented smile on his face. 'This woman has been wearing me out—night after night enticing me into bed early and not taking no for an answer!'

Greg smiled. 'Well, it certainly paid off.'

'Maybe that's what was wrong before. We weren't getting together often enough,' Chris said, grinning broadly.

'Obviously,' Fiona replied quickly, turning to smile at Lindy with a barely perceptible wink.

What a performance! Lindy thought—to be able to tell white lies like that. But wasn't that what she was doing herself—living a lie in front of Greg?

She turned away, aware that his quizzical eyes were on her. The nagging voice inside her head was repeating Fiona's phrase from earlier in the morning—'He has a right to know.' She would tell Greg Fiona's secret, but she could never tell him her own.

She was clearing her desk at the end of the morning session when he came in to see her. Rona was folding sheets in the examination cubicle.

Greg asked Rona to finish off and leave them alone.

Lindy frowned as the door closed behind her staff nurse.

'Again, I'd like to know if that was necessary,' she said in her most professional tone. She wasn't going to let him accuse her of losing her temper but she objected to him marching in and ordering her staff around.

He towered above her. 'Of course it was, and you know why.'

Her heart started to pound unnervingly. 'I'm sure I don't know what you're talking about.'

He leaned against her desk, too close for comfort; she was aware of his muscular thighs straining against the immaculate, expensive cloth of his ever so eminent surgeon's suit.

She focused her eyes on the subtle stripes of his grey silk shirt, studiously avoiding eye contact.

'Why don't you stop keeping this secret all to yourself?' he began testily. 'Come on, out with it, Lindy. I wasn't born yesterday. You and Fiona were hatching something and—'

'Yes, yes, it's OK,' she said, inwardly breathing a sigh of relief. 'Fiona gave me her permission to tell you. She said you had a right to know. Those were her exact words.'

For a few nerve-racking seconds she'd thought that Greg was speaking on a personal level. She paused to catch her breath before outlining Fiona's deception and the need for continuing secrecy. While she was speaking Greg got up from the desk and began to pace the room, pausing to stare out of the window with his back to her. She could feel the tension increasing between them.

'Greg, you see why I couldn't tell you before, don't you?' she said nervously, after seconds had elapsed and there had been no response to her revelations.

When he turned around his face was an enigmatic mask, but she could tell by the increased pace of his breathing that he was moved. He came towards her and leaned once more against the desk, his hands tightly gripping the edge.

'The situation we have between Chris and Fiona is not as uncommon as you would imagine,' he said evenly. 'The lengths some women go to to keep a secret from their husband never fail to amaze me. I mean, if you're in a good partnership, surely you should be able to discuss everything?'

'Did you discuss everything with your wife?' Lindy asked boldly.

He gave a wry smile. 'Yes, I did. . .at first. I thought we had no secrets. Which was why it was all the harder when I found out she was deceiving me. . .for the second time. There was no question of me wanting to continue in the relationship after that.'

'The second time?' Linda queried. 'You mean she'd had another love affair?'

He hesitated. 'Possibly; I don't know. The deception that really hit me was when Jane and I were trying for a baby and I discovered, quite by chance, she was still on the Pill. When I challenged her she said she didn't want children but she knew I did so she'd pretended to go along with the idea.'

Lindy swallowed hard. It was certainly a day for

opening up old wounds. 'So what did you decide to do?' she asked gently.

'We were still trying to sort that one out when I discovered she was having an affair. I desperately wanted to start a family and I thought Jane would come round to my way of thinking in time.'

He ran a hand through his hair, frowning in concentration as he recalled the past.

'I was an only child of older, academic parents who'd put off having children while they pursued their university careers. They both died when I was in my teens. I thought having a family would be the most wonderful experience. . .I still do, with the right woman. . .at the right time.'

Lindy remained silent. After a few seconds she raised her eyes to his. The expression on his face was wistful, and she was alarmed at the pangs of jealousy that began to stab her. She really hated the woman who'd betrayed Greg, and at the same time she was envious of the love they'd shared. Jane and Greg had experienced a full-blown relationship—lived together, laughed together, made love together. . .

'So you see why I walked out on my wife and her lover that day,' he said quietly. 'At the time I felt as if she'd destroyed everything we'd worked for together. She'd made a complete mockery of our marriage and I never wanted to trust a woman again. Wouldn't any man have done the same?'

Her pulses raced as she hesitated. 'You shouldn't have gone out in such an unstable condition and walked into my life,' she blurted out.

He walked round the desk, grasped her hands and pulled her to her feet. 'Was it so awful, that night we spent together?'

His warm breath was fanning her face. His mouth was hovering somewhere above her forehead, his tantalising lips forming words that rocked her in the most evocative way. She ought to move out of the circle of his arms but she felt powerless against the charismatic pull he exerted over her.

'You know it wasn't,' she heard herself whisper. 'You know how—'

But he didn't let her finish. His lips swooped down to crush hers. She felt herself opening up to him, and there was nothing she could do to quell the sensual vibrations running down her spine as his tongue lingered against hers. This was how it had been on that fateful night; she'd loved every kiss, every caress, every time he'd taken her.

He was pulling himself away, running his hands once more through his rumpled hair as if making an attempt to return to professional normality.

'I thought you'd changed, Lindy,' he said huskily. 'But you haven't.'

'Oh, but I have,' she said quietly. 'Nothing will ever be the same again.'

'Let me know when you're ready to talk about it,' he said.

She gave him a startled glance.

'This secret you're keeping from me. When you're ready to share it, I'll be ready to listen. Until then, we'll keep the platonic flag flying, shall we? Have you checked your diary yet?'

'Haven't had a minute this morning, as well you know.'

She was brisk and to the point, trying to suppress the fluttering of the butterflies in the pit of her tummy. 'My diary's in my bag here somewhere.'

She found it and gave it a cursory glance, suddenly not wanting Greg to see what a quiet life she was leading at the moment. She realised that, apart from her work, she'd been holding herself free for any engagements that might crop up on the spur of the moment. She'd wondered so often how she would cope if Greg asked her out. Her firm intention had been to say no, but now. . .

'Yes, tomorrow night's OK,' she said, closing the diary decisively.

He was watching her with a whimsical smile. 'Well, I'm sorry to take up your time with such a boring occasion—a lot of old fogeys jigging around in evening dress. But maybe we'll liven things up. And we could always go on somewhere afterwards.'

'That would be nice,' she heard herself say.

He put a finger under her chin, tilting her face upwards so that she had to reveal the expression of longing that she was trying to hide.

'There's hope for us yet,' he whispered.

The door was opening.

'Oh, sorry, sir; I thought you would have finished your discussion by now,' Rona said, suppressing a knowing grin.

For once Lindy didn't mind the innuendo, but as she watched Greg leaving she wondered how she would be able to guess when his advances were real or put on for effect. Their relationship was now far too complicated for her liking, and she could feel herself becoming more and more involved.

CHAPTER FIVE

THE following morning, while Lindy was getting ready for a full session in her consulting room in the infertility clinic, her concentration continually wavered as she thought about the evening ahead. Before coming on duty she'd made a quick scan of her wardrobe and decided that she had absolutely nothing she could possibly wear to a grand function like the board of governors banquet. Greg had told her that he was obliged to go in an evening suit and black tie, but he thought that she'd be able to get away with a smart cocktail dress.

Smart cocktail dress! she thought as she pulled open the case notes of her first patient. Where did Greg think she would have got the money for something like that?

Rona put another couple of files on her desk and stayed to chat.

'What are you going to wear tonight?'

Lindy groaned. 'Don't ask. I'm planning a quick dash round Moortown this afternoon, but I don't suppose I can afford anything suitable.'

She swivelled her chair round; for once she welcomed a chat with her faithful staff nurse.

'You've lived in Moortown all your life haven't you, Rona? Where would you advise me to start looking for a smart cocktail dress, if such a thing still exists?'

'Oh, it certainly does exist in this neck of the woods,' Rona said, sitting down in the patients' chair, ready to revel in a girly discussion. 'People dress up in Moortown if they get the chance and the Board of

Governors Banquet will be a really smart occasion.'

'Thanks very much,' Lindy said drily. 'Well, come on, advise me where to get this dressy little number.'

'The charity shop,' Rona said without hesitation. 'Either that or the Good As New boutique in the high street. The charity shop won't have such a big selection but they'll be cheaper than Good As New. The Moortown ladies who lunch and dine hate to be seen in the same thing twice, so they donate their cast-offs to charity or sell them for a small fee to the Good As New.'

Lindy smiled. 'Rona, you're brilliant! I would never have thought of that.'

Rona smiled back, obviously enjoying the compliment. 'How are things between you and Greg?'

Lindy swivelled her chair back again to face the desk and picked up the case notes of the first patient. 'About the same,' she said tonelessly. 'See if Maria Thomson has arrived, will you, Rona?'

Lindy concentrated on the notes as Rona went out to look for the patient. Rona's expression seemed to indicate that she was reluctant to curtail the gossip that hadn't been as revealing as she'd hoped.

That's the trouble with confiding in Rona, Lindy thought. As soon as you tell her one thing she starts up the inquisition. Still, it was good to find out about the clothes shops. There wouldn't be much time to spare during the afternoon if she was to clear her work for an early-evening getaway.

'Mrs Thomson, do come in and sit down,' Lindy said as Rona ushered in her small, dark-haired patient. 'May I call you Maria?'

The patient smiled and nodded. 'I'd like that, Doctor.'

'Let me see, the last time I saw you was a couple of months ago when we did some microsurgery to unblock your Fallopian tubes. You went home at the end of January and—'

'And success!' The patient was grinning from ear to ear.

Lindy leaned forward, smiling. 'I'm having a really good week with my patients. You're the second success story in two days. Are you just guessing or have you done a pregnancy test, Maria?'

'I've done a test—in fact several—to make sure! I can't believe it, after all this time. It's like a miracle.'

'We like to have satisfied clients in this department,' Lindy said. 'I'll put a call through to Dr Dalton; he performed your operation and he'll be delighted to know it was successful.'

'That's good news,' she heard Greg say at the other end of the phone. 'I'll come across in a few minutes when I've got a break between patients.'

While they were waiting for Greg Lindy did a full examination and concluded that the pregnancy was about six weeks on.

'You didn't waste much time, Maria,' Greg said, smiling as he came through into the examination cubicle. 'That's what I like—patients who are totally committed to obeying doctor's orders.'

'I can't thank you enough, Doctor,' Maria said, reaching out to take hold of Greg's hand. 'It really is a miracle. I'd completely lost hope and we were considering adoption.'

'We'll have you transferred to the antenatal department now,' Greg said. 'They'll take care of you, but we'll keep in touch and try to be around when you come in to have your baby. I'll make a note of the expected date of arrival. I know it's a long way ahead but time simply flies around here. I'll be around and, hopefully, Dr Cash will too, but we can't be sure of that.'

He looked down at Maria and added by way of explanation, 'There may be some staff changes here.'

Lindy felt the apprehension rising inside her. She wished that Greg wouldn't keep reminding her that she was still here on probation, as it were. One wrong move and she'd be out on her ear!

'One week to the end of my year in the house, Greg,' she said quietly as their patient was getting dressed in the cubicle. 'Would it be foolish to start counting my chickens?'

Greg leaned across Lindy's desk. 'Difficult to predict. I'd say you stand more of a chance now than you did three months ago. Brad seemed pleased the last time we discussed you.'

Lindy mentally counted up to ten before she spoke. 'I hate to think of you two weighing me up like a candidate in a school exam,' she said, half under her breath so that Maria wouldn't hear.

'Oh, there's far more at stake than you imagine, Lindy,' Greg said as he went out of the door. 'Just don't take anything for granted.'

She held back the retort that sprang to her lips. She wanted this job more than anything, so she would have to toe the line.

During the rest of the morning Lindy had no time to worry about the problems of her career, or her relationship with Greg. She grabbed a quick sandwich in the canteen before heading for the Moortown shops.

As she immersed herself in the shopping expedition she tried desperately to forget Greg's words but they kept coming back to her. 'More at stake than you imagine', he'd said. That sounded ominous. Maybe she'd been over-confident about this job. Perhaps the pseudo-affair had been a useless exercise. Was this evening out a farewell gesture before the board of governors put the knife in and told her that she wasn't suitable for the job that she'd thought was in the bag before Greg had arrived?

As she stood in front of the Good As New shop in the high street, staring at the window display, the unwelcome ideas tumbling through her head, she drew in her breath and gave a big sigh.

'Problems, Lindy?' said a female voice.

'Sara!' Lindy put on a smile for the benefit of the friend and colleague who was feeding the parking meter in front of the shop. 'You're not looking for a dress, are you?'

'Certainly am,' Sara replied, joining Lindy to gaze through the wide plate-glass window. 'Nothing fits me any more; I'm nearly four months and pregnancy is playing havoc with my waistline. I'm going to look like a little barrel during the summer months.'

Lindy smiled down at the diminutive Sara. It was true that she looked a little thicker around the waist but she still retained her attractive elfin face and slim limbs.

'I thought consultants' wives wouldn't be seen dead in a second-hand dress,' Lindy said.

Sara laughed. 'You must be joking! We're just as hard up as the rest of the medical profession. I'm considering being a full-time mum for a few years; we'll have to manage on one salary so I'm starting as I mean to go on. And the wedding in a couple of weeks is going to be an expensive affair. My parents are insisting on all the trimmings so Brad and I are helping out financially. Mum and Dad couldn't possibly foot the bill now they're retired and living off a fixed income.

'Come on, let's go inside and see what we can find. At least we won't fight over the same dress, you being so tall and slim, and me being short and getting podgier by the minute.'

'I'm looking forward to the wedding,' Lindy said as they went up a couple of worn stone steps and in through the quaint, old-fashioned doorway. A bell rang as the door opened and closed.

'You won't have any problem getting up to the Lake District for our wedding, will you, Lindy?' Sara asked as they waited for someone to appear. 'Will Greg drive you up there?'

'I'll probably go by myself,' Lindy said quickly. 'I know the area quite well. I've got an old schoolfriend who lives up there; I stayed with her before I came to Moortown. Greg, being the newcomer to the hospital, has said he'll probably stay behind and hold the fort.'

'Well, Greg may have been here only a couple of months but Brad considers he's a good friend already, and we were both hoping he'd be there,' Sara said. 'But I suppose he'll decide what's best for the department. We can't have the whole of Moortown General on leave of absence.'

A tall, imposing, middle-aged lady swept in from the back of the shop in a swirl of Jaeger and pearls.

'Dr Clarkson,' she said, smiling amiably at Sara. 'What a pleasure to see you again. I hear congratulations are in order.'

'Do you mean the wedding or the pitter-patter of tiny feet, Mrs Holt?' asked Sara, with a mischievous grin.

'Oh—er—I was meaning the wedding, my dear. I didn't know that—'

'That's why I'm here,' Sara interrupted. 'I'm suffering from thickening of the waistline—a medical condition that won't go away until at least September in my case, so I may be calling in more often during the summer. The pressing problem is the Board of Governors Banquet tonight. My colleague, Dr Cash, is going to the same event, so we both need fixing up.'

'Tonight? Good heavens! Left it a bit late haven't you, ladies?'

Mrs Holt began running her hands along a dress rack marked with the words 'After Six'.

'The sizings are difficult to gauge when we have such a lot of foreign designer clothing.'

'Nothing too expensive, Mrs Holt,' Sara put in cautiously.

Lindy tried on a cream silk suit but it was too big. She twirled in front of the mirror in the middle of the shop bemoaning the fact that it looked like a tent on her.

'I used to be a size twelve but I've lost weight since I joined the new department. Have you got anything like this in a ten, Mrs Holt?'

The lady of the shop shook her head. 'We could have had it taken in if there'd been more time. How about this black one? Black's always smart and it would go well with your red hair and green eyes.'

Lindy tried on a black taffeta dress that reached to mid-calf. She nipped the waist in with the belt that came with it. Mrs Holt draped a red silk rose across the low neckline and Lindy nodded.

'Yes, I like this one.'

'I should think so too. You look gorgeous,' Sara said a trifle enviously. 'I wish I had long, slim legs like you. What do you think of this pink chiffon? Does it make me look like the dumpy fairy on the top of the Christmas tree, Lindy?'

'The dropped waistline is a good idea in your condition,' Mrs Holt told Sara.

Sara nodded. 'That's what I thought. Can't do with anything tight. OK, that's me fixed up.'

Lindy was pleasantly surprised at the price of her dress.

'I'll definitely come here again,' she told Sara as they went out into the street.

'You can come back tomorrow and sell it back to Mrs Holt, or are you planning to go to more of these stuffy functions with Greg?' Sara asked.

'I wish you wouldn't keep pairing me off with Greg!' Lindy said.

The effort of keeping up the pretence in front of her friend had finally got to her. As soon as she'd snapped she felt contrite. She'd got no right to take it out on someone else.

'I'm sorry, Sara. I didn't mean to be rude but the strain of—' She stopped in mid-sentence.

Sara put her hand on Lindy's arm. 'That's OK. You've been working too hard. Brad keeps telling me what a good job you're doing in the infertility clinic. You stand a very good chance of being chosen for the job when you've finished your stint in the house.'

'Do you think so?'

Sara hesitated. 'It's not for me to say. It's up to Brad and Greg. . .and the board of governors, of course. But why did you say I shouldn't pair you with Greg? I thought things were going smoothly between the two of you. Brad was beginning to think that you two running the clinic as a couple would be ideal. Have you had a tiff or something?'

'No,' Lindy replied quickly.

So Greg's idea of a liaison between them had been a good idea after all! But how long could she keep up the pretence before she cracked? And did she want to keep pretending?

'I like to keep my independence when I'm working with Greg, that's all. I hate to feel he's taking me over, even though he is the boss.'

Sara smiled. 'I think I know what you mean. . .but I won't repeat anything you've said to Brad.'

Lindy smiled back. 'Thanks. I'd appreciate that, because I really do want this job, Sara.'

'Like I said, you're in with a very good chance. Can I give you a lift anywhere?'

'No, thanks. I've got some more shopping to do.'

'See you tonight,' Sara said as she opened her car door.

Lindy dashed along the high street into Marks and Spencer for black tights, lacy pants and a strapless bra. She'd decided that the dress was cut too low for her to wear a normal bra.

She walked back to hospital, calling in at her room to dump her purchases before spending the rest of the afternoon on Nightingale with her obstetric patients in the mother and baby unit.

She was delighted to meet up with one of her long-term patients. Gwendoline Brown had experienced several medical problems, first in conceiving and then in holding onto the pregnancy. A tiny, premature baby boy of three and a half pounds had just been delivered by James Dewhirst and the staff midwives when Lindy arrived in the prem unit, and Gwendoline's gratitude was very touching.

Here was a baby who hadn't been expected to survive during the pregnancy; there had been several occasions when a miscarriage had threatened, but by caring for Gwendoline each time in hospital Lindy had kept the pregnancy going until thirty-six weeks.

'Well done, Gwen,' Lindy said, pulling up a chair to sit beside her patient while she checked on the medication and progress charts.

Gwen Brown lay back against the pillows and gave a big sigh.

'I'm glad that's over, Dr Cash. I feel so tired, but you've all been so wonderful. Have you seen Darren yet? He's so small! I've never seen such a tiny baby.'

'I'm just on my way to the prem unit, Gwen, to see him. Dr Dewhirst is with your baby at the moment.'

Lindy examined Gwen when she'd finished writing up the medication and treatment charts.

'No problems there, Gwen,' she said. 'What you need now is a rest. We'll take care of Darren while you get some sleep.'

In the prem unit Lindy found James Dewhirst setting up a saline drip on baby Darren.

'I tried to get him to take something by mouth but he's too weak,' he explained. 'So this is the only way I can get some fluids into him. I'll ask the night staff to discontinue this and try him with a feed in a few hours when he should be a bit stronger. I've got to go to the Board of Governors Banquet but the staff will cope here. Are you on call this evening, Lindy?'

She smiled. 'On call but also out at the Board of Governors Banquet.'

'I thought it was just for registrars and consultants. . . Oops, sorry! I expect you're going with Greg, aren't you?'

Lindy kept the smile glued to her face. 'Yes, that's right. I'm sure the night staff will keep a careful watch on baby Darren. I'd like to take a look at him now, James.'

James Dewhirst went on to the next little patient, leaving Lindy to examine the tiny prem and draw her own conclusions. He seemed healthy enough apart from his low weight, which was to be expected. But the wizened, old-man expression on his newborn face was particularly pronounced, as if he was suffering some kind of internal pain. She gently palpated the tiny abdomen, and the baby gave a howl of protest.

'I think we should have young Darren X-rayed in the morning, when he's a bit stronger, James,' she suggested to her colleague. 'There's a definite tender spot here in the epigastric region and a slight lump over the pylorus at the exit from his tummy.'

James agreed. 'We'll schedule it for first thing tomorrow.'

'I'd like to keep an eye on Darren for the next few days,' Lindy said. 'I've known him since he was a flashing light on the ultrasound screen so I'm very fond of him already.'

'You sound broody,' James said, with a wry smile.

'That'll be the day!' Lindy retorted. 'I like other people's babies. The sort you can hand back.'

Did she really mean that? she thought as she went off duty. Had the reaction to her miscarriage made her so hard that she couldn't contemplate another pregnancy or the possibility that she might have a baby in the future? Greg had said that he longed to have a family. . .with the right woman. . .at the right time. Wouldn't another baby help to heal the wound of losing the first?

She ran down the steps that led to the residents' corridor, trying to shake off the compelling ideas in her head. There were so many hurdles to get over before she could even begin to think along these lines. She had no reason to believe that Greg was even fond of her. A one-night stand had been followed three months later by a shouting match on the transatlantic phone, followed by a twenty-month silence, followed by two months of working together in a constant state of tension and mismatch, interspersed with brief occasions when he'd set her pulses racing again.

Yes, in spite of everything she was still attracted to Greg, but how did he feel about her? And how would he feel if he knew that she hadn't told him about their baby? Would he be furious? Knowing him as she did now, she was sure of it! He'd been devastated when he'd found out that his wife was deceiving him about being on the Pill, so he wasn't likely to forgive Lindy for holding out on him about the baby she'd lost. It had been his baby too. He would be sure to insist that he'd had a right to know about it.

Back in her room she closed the door and leaned against it, breathing deeply to control the emotions that threatened to engulf her again. She'd got to get a grip on herself before she met Greg tonight. She'd got to be in control.

A shower helped to calm and relax her. The new bra and pants put her in a more luxurious mood; by the time she'd zipped up the black dress, which gave just a peep of mid-calf and ankle, she was in charge of herself again. In fact she was in total control for a full half-hour, until she heard Greg knocking on the door.

She looked in the full-length mirror and told herself that now wasn't the time to fall to pieces. She'd gone to great lengths to look her best.

'Wow! You look stunning!' Greg stood in the doorway, admiration shining in his dark, expressive eyes.

'Thanks, you look quite good yourself,' she said, thinking that 'quite good' was a total understatement for the handsome, dress-suited man in front of her. The racing of her pulses was setting in again.

'Well, let's not waste any time,' Greg said. 'Your carriage awaits, *madame*.'

'Hold on a minute while I get a jacket. I can leave it in the car, can't I? I don't possess anything grand enough to hand in at the cloakroom.'

She sat very still in the passenger seat as Greg drove out through the hospital gates. This was the first time that she'd been in his sleek black Mercedes and she was enjoying the distinctive aroma of leather and luxury. It was a totally different experience from driving along in her ancient blue Mini—which, she thought suddenly, she really must get around to cleaning some time, outside and especially inside, removing things like combs, discarded lipsticks worn to the end, and empty tissue-boxes.

'You're very quiet, Lindy.' Greg kept his eyes on the road as he drove through Moortown.

She gave a nervous chuckle. 'To be honest, I'm over-awed, and we haven't even got there. All those stuffed shirts and their ladies. What on earth shall we have in common?'

He laughed. 'Absolutely nothing! But it won't matter; you're with me, and after the initial socialising we can do our own thing. Find a quiet corner with a bottle of champagne.'

She felt the colour rising in her cheeks as the implication hit her forcefully.

'I don't expect there'll be a quiet corner at this sort of occasion,' she said quickly.

'There's sure to be a corner, and maybe we won't notice the noise,' he said evenly.

'Don't, Greg,' she whispered, half under her breath. 'Don't try to dredge up the past.'

'I was thinking of the future,' he replied, taking his eyes for a split second from the road.

Her heart seemed to give a somersault. 'How about concentrating on the present?' she said. 'The past is over and I don't want to worry about the future. I may not have a job after tonight if I say the wrong thing to the wrong dignitary.'

He was pulling into the civic hall car park, having shown his ticket to the car-park attendant on the gate.

She waited in the car until he came round to open her door and hold out his hand to help her out. She'd discarded the old jacket, and even though the April evening was mild she shivered as they hurried up the wide stone steps into the high-ceilinged entrance hall.

'Dr Gregory Dalton and Dr Lindy Cash,' intoned the Master of Ceremonies at the entrance to the banqueting hall.

She was aware of crystal chandeliers twinkling above her, snatches of gossip all around her from the well-heeled crowd, glasses clinking.

A waiter with a tray appeared in front of them and Greg took two glasses.

'We've got the champagne,' he said, handing her a fizzing glass. 'All we need now is the quiet corner.'

'Dr Dalton, what a pleasure to see you again!'

An elderly, white-haired man was reaching out to grasp Greg's hand.

'This is Sir Jack Hamilton, our chairman of the board,' Greg said. 'Dr Lindy Cash.'

As Lindy shook hands with the pink-cheeked, rotund little man she was aware that he was scrutinising every detail of her appearance.

'I didn't have the pleasure of meeting you when you came for your interview here, Dr Cash. House surgeons are appointed by the internal medical staff. The board is only called in for the more exalted positions such as the one I believe you're being considered for at the moment.'

Sir Jack Hamilton was still holding her hand. Gently she withdrew her fingers so that he wouldn't notice how tense she felt when the new job was discussed.

'You're very young, my dear, and relatively inexperienced, although I'm told you've been working hard in our new clinic. There were a few teething problems, I believe—' He broke off to give a wry smile at Greg before continuing. 'But that's all been ironed out and we seem to have a near-perfect arrangement. A married couple in charge of our infertility unit would be ideal. I hadn't hoped—'

'I think you've misunderstood, sir,' Lindy interrupted hastily.

'Oh, I don't think so,' the chairman continued relentlessly. 'Maybe it's not common knowledge yet, but a little bird told me that perhaps in the near future we might be having a hat trick in the Moortown obstetrics department. I'm referring to Hannah and Simon Delaware, Sara and Brad, and now—'

'With the greatest respect, sir,' Lindy put in firmly, 'I think, possibly, you're jumping to conclusions. And now, if you'll excuse me. . .'

Lindy saw the frown on the chairman's face as she walked away, back towards the corridor.

'Lindy!' Greg's hand was on her waist. 'You can't just walk out like this.'

She had reached the door. The touch of Greg's fingers was calming her but the emotional turmoil deep down inside was still there.

'Come outside with me for a few minutes, Greg. We have to talk,' she said quietly.

She turned away from the oncoming crowd of new arrivals and walked along a wide, stone-flagged corridor to the back of the building, going through a door that led to a small garden. She didn't notice the difference in temperature—from the hot, stuffy hall to the fresh evening air—as she walked outside and sank down onto a wooden seat facing a small pond illuminated with multicoloured fairy lights.

Greg sat down beside her, his arm on the back of the seat.

'You shouldn't have done that,' he said evenly. 'Sir Jack Hamilton has a lot of influence and—'

'Greg, I can't go on living a lie. You and I both know this pseudo-relationship won't work. Sooner or later we're going to have to break it up, and it might as well be sooner.

'You're good at deception but I'm not. The night we met I had absolutely no idea that you were married. You fooled me completely. But I can't go on pretending there's something going on between us when there isn't. And if this job depends on living a lie then I don't want it. I want to be appointed on my own merit, not because you and I would make a good professional couple.'

He pulled her into his arms and began to stroke the back of her hair. She remained very still.

'We would make a good professional couple, Lindy,' he said gently. 'We'd also be very good together off duty. . .if only you'd come clean about what's troubling you. You said I was good at deception but you're the one who's holding out on me. Why is it that the women in my life refuse to be honest with me?'

She stiffened as she looked up into his eyes. In the half-light she could see his hurt expression, and the deep-seated guilt inside her rose to the surface. If she came clean, told him about the baby, how would he react? She shivered.

'You're cold,' he murmured. 'Here, put this on.'

As he enveloped her in his dinner jacket she could smell his distinctive aftershave; she felt the warmth of his body still lingering on the material.

'We could have a real future together, Lindy,' he whispered, his voice husky with emotion.

She lifted her face towards his. 'One step at a time, Greg. Let's not rush things.'

He kissed her gently on the lips. 'As I said the other day, there's hope for us yet.'

'But not while the whole hospital is holding its breath waiting for an announcement,' she said quietly, her senses still reeling from the touch of his lips. 'I want to get to know you, Greg, before. . .before we make up our minds about whether—'

'Lindy, thank goodness I've found you!' James Dewhirst, looking totally transformed in his evening suit, was running down the path towards them.

'Someone said they'd seen you heading this way. Could you do me a really big favour?' He rushed on without waiting for a reply. 'I've just had a message from the hospital about our newly delivered prem, Darren Brown. Night Sister tried to give him a feed and he vomited immediately in a projectile way. That coupled with the tenderness over the abdomen—'

'A possible pyloric stenosis,' Lindy put in. 'I had my suspicions after I examined Darren this afternoon.'

James nodded. 'So I think someone should go back and check him out, and possibly operate tonight. The thing is, I'm told I've got an emergency Caesarean in Theatre One in an hour and—'

'I'll go back with Lindy; we'll take Theatre Two if we decide to operate on the little chap,' Greg said quickly.

Lindy was on her feet, Greg's arm still around her; James Dewhirst, looking from one to the other, exclaimed, 'Thanks very much! What a useful couple you are!'

'Yes, aren't we?' said Greg, smiling at James.

'We're stuck with it now,' Lindy whispered as they made their way down the corridor towards the front door.

'Just keeping everyone guessing,' Greg replied.

'Does that include me?' she said.

For a moment he stopped and pulled her around to face him. She was very much aware that his jacket was still draped around her shoulders. He took hold of the lapels and drew her towards him.

'I won't keep you guessing, Lindy,' he said huskily. 'You can always tell when it's for real.'

Her heart did a big somersault. What an ambiguous

remark! She thought as they continued on their way. She felt even more confused thar before. But one thing was for sure—she could feel herself falling more and more hopelessly in love.

'Good evening, Greg!' Brad called from the main entrance, where he and Sara along with Hannah and Simon were just arriving.

Lindy pulled the jacket from her shoulders and handed it to Greg.

'You're not leaving, are you?' Sara asked as they all met by the door.

'One of our patients on Nightingale, Brad,' Lindy explained. 'Darren Brown, the prem that James delivered this afternoon. There's a possibility he may have pyloric stenosis. I'll go and take a look at him. Greg's coming with me.'

'Sure you don't mind, Greg?' Brad asked. 'After all, he's my patient.'

Greg smiled. 'No need to drag our illustrious consultant along. If I think his operation can't wait, I'll go ahead with it.'

'Thanks a lot. Keep me informed.'

'Pity you didn't have a chance to show off your dress, Lindy,' Sara said. 'Such a waste!'

Greg put his arm around Lindy's shoulders and drew her away down the stone stairs.

'It wasn't wasted,' he whispered. 'I appreciated it. I've never seen you look so stunning.'

Inside the car he pulled her towards him and kissed her tenderly on the lips. There was no passion in the kiss. It was as light as a butterfly's wing but it moved Lindy more than any of his previous kisses. There was a new warmth, a genuine feeling of intimacy.

Was this the beginning of a real affair between them?

CHAPTER SIX

NIGHTINGALE WARD was shrouded in semi-darkness when Greg and Lindy arrived. Night Sister Eva Sharp, a recently appointed, forty-something sister, who had returned to nursing now that her family had grown up, filled them in on the details of the case and found clean white coats for them to put over their evening dress.

'Sorry to drag you away from the banquet,' she said.

'Don't worry,' Lindy said. 'I'm very fond of little Darren. I've known him almost as long as his mum has. You say he did a projectile vomit on his first feed?'

Eva Sharp nodded. 'It shot out in front of me in the typical way that I've seen with babies who have a blockage at the exit from the stomach.'

'Yes. So, coupled with the examination that Dr Cash did this afternoon, it would seem we have a case of pyloric stenosis on our hands, Sister,' Greg said. 'Will you call Theatre Two and have the staff standing by in case we decide to operate tonight?'

In the prem unit baby Darren was crying. Lindy picked him up, sat him on her lap and put a practised finger gently over the region of the abdomen; there was no doubt about it—she could feel a small lump over the pylorus.

'Feel that, Greg,' she said, removing her finger.

A couple of seconds later he nodded. 'That's not going to go away. We'd better get the poor little lamb into theatre.'

Eva stepped in to prepare Darren for theatre while Greg and Lindy went along to scrub up and change into theatre greens in the ante-theatre.

A small team was waiting for them in Theatre Two. Lindy looked down at the tiny, motionless form on the table under the bright lights.

'Scalpel, please, Lindy,' Greg said.

He made a small incision in the skin of the baby's abdomen before explaining that he was going to do a classic Ramstedt's operation.

'Is there anybody who hasn't seen one before?' He glanced briefly around the team.

Rachel Nutford, a young student nurse on her first night duty, said from the back of the theatre that she hadn't.

'OK; well, come a bit nearer, Nurse, and I'll explain what I'm doing. At the moment I'm cutting through the thin abdominal wall to expose the baby's stomach.'

A few minutes later Greg pointed out where the muscles controlling the sphincter at the exit from the stomach were clenched so tightly that nothing could pass through.

'This means I've got to divide up the muscle fibres so that there is a workable opening between the stomach and the duodenum—the start of the small intestine.'

At the end of the operation Lindy stayed with baby Darren in the recovery room that led off from one side of the theatre. She was relieved when he came round from the anaesthetic and began wailing loudly.

'Nothing wrong with his lungs,' Greg said, coming back into the room. 'Let's have a look at the wound.'

'No problems there,' Lindy said. 'Slightly raised pulse but his temperature is normal.'

Sister Sharp arrived to take Darren back to the prem unit.

'Continue the glucose and saline drip, Sister; we'll start feeding by mouth in about four hours. I've written out the feeding chart. It will be 5ml of five per cent glucose in water every hour for the first four feeds, increasing to 7-8ml for the next four. Bradley Prestcot will, no doubt, be in to see Darren tomorrow and give you further instructions. If you're worried in the night you'd better get the switchboard to contact Mr Prestcot, and he'll arrange for someone to come and help you.'

'Or you can call me,' Lindy said.

'You're not going back to the banquet, then?' Sister said. 'It's barely midnight. Doesn't it go on till two?'

Greg smiled. 'It certainly does, but I'm not going to struggle back into my penguin suit. How about you, Lindy? Do you want to dress up again?'

'No fear! I'm going to bed. Goodnight, Sister.'

Greg walked along to the separate male and female staff cloakrooms, where they'd left their evening clothes. Both emerged seconds later with clothes draped over their arms.

Lindy pulled her theatre cap off and tossed it into the laundry bin.

'I feel decidedly scruffy in these theatre greens,' she said as they went down the steps leading to the residents' quarters. 'Can't wait to get into the shower.'

'Can you wait long enough to have a coffee with me?' Greg said.

She hesitated. 'Give me ten minutes to shower and I'll be with you.'

Back in her room she hung the posh frock on a hanger. Her spirits rose as she began to think that there was a distinct possibility that she might use it again. She felt like Cinderella who'd been dragged home early from the ball, but the prospect of a quiet coffee with Greg was infinitely more appealing than tripping the light fantastic at the Board of Governors Banquet.

The hot water cascaded over her; she doused herself liberally with shower gel. Feeling refreshed, she stepped out of the shower, rolling up the theatre greens to take back in the morning.

There was a delicious aroma of ground coffee when Greg opened his door. His eyes lingered over her newly pressed jeans and freshly laundered cotton shirt.

'Mmm, you smell good,' he said, nuzzling his face into her still-damp hair before dropping a kiss on the side of her cheek. 'Now we can relax and get to know each other. You did say you wanted to get to know me, didn't you, Dr Cash?'

Lindy laughed. This was much better! The animosity had disappeared. She could pretend that they were two people who'd just met; there were no hang-ups from the past, no reason why they shouldn't get together; there was no guilt. . . Ah, she wasn't sure about that. It was difficult to forget that until she told Greg about their baby she was keeping a secret from him. But, for the umpteenth time, she wondered nervously how he would react if she told him.

'How do you take your coffee?'

'Black,' she said quickly.

'It's strange that I have to ask you, because you'd think I would have found that out in the two years and one month since we first met,' he said as he handed her a cup and then lounged back against the other end of the sofa where she was sitting.

She looked across at him and felt a surge of excitement. He was wearing a navy blue fisherman's jersey and hip-hugging jeans; a broad leather belt was fastened over his taut waist with a brass buckle. He

looked more than usually handsome in the half-light
provided by discreetly placed table lamps.

Over at one end of the room she could see floor-
length curtains that shut out the prying eyes of the rest
of the hospital. Soft feather cushions were scattered
over the sofa and armchairs. The carpet had a deep
mushroom pile.

'This room doesn't look like hospital issue,' she said.
'Did you furnish it yourself?'

He hesitated. 'It wasn't difficult. Jane didn't want
any of our old furniture when she moved in with Bob,
so I put it in storage. When I came to Moortown I
had it delivered up here.'

She felt herself cringing away from the sofa. Was
this where Greg and his wife had sat together. . .
maybe made love together?

As if reading her mind, Greg said, 'But I started
afresh with the furniture in my cottage.'

'Ah, yes, the pink house,' Lindy said. 'Do you get
there very often?'

'As often as I can. You haven't been to see
me there.'

She met his eyes. 'Haven't been invited. . .recently.'

'As I recall, you turned down my invitation to look
the place over way back in February. We'll have to
do something about that. We could, of course, drive
over there now.'

Her heart began to throb madly. 'What about our
postoperative prem?'

'He's Brad's patient. His registrar, James Dewhirst,
should have finished his emergency Caesarean by now,
and Brian Mason, your fellow house surgeon, is a com-
petent young man.'

'Not tonight,' Lindy said. She hesitated. 'It's
too soon.'

'Too soon for what?' he asked, with a wry grin. 'Too

soon for us to be alone in what could turn out to be a compromising situation? That's not what you said a couple of years ago.'

'I wasn't thinking clearly. It was all a mistake. . .' Her voice trailed away as she saw the hurt expression in his eyes.

'So you told me on the phone,' he said evenly. 'It didn't seem like a mistake at the time. I was disappointed when you didn't return to hospital in London when you were due back from holiday. I made enquiries and they told me you'd resigned. That was when I got your phone number in the States and gave you a call. Your mother answered and said you were in hospital. So what made you decide to work in a hospital out there instead of coming back to the UK?'

'I just changed my mind, that's all,' she said glibly, hating herself for the deception. But she didn't want to go into the details tonight just when the ice was beginning to melt. She wanted everything to be as it had been on that first night.

'Woman's privilege to change her mind, so they say; but when I called back you were definitely out of order. Screaming down the phone and telling me to go away—'

'I was ill the night you phoned. . .Yes, I remember; I was feeling awful.'

He reached across and pulled her into his arms. 'Must have been some illness,' he said gently. 'I wish you'd told me.'

She took a deep breath as she looked up into those dark eyes that she'd come to love so much. She also was wishing that she'd told him then; the longer she left it, the worse it became.

She knew how he hated deception in a woman; he hated his ex-wife for what she'd done to him, for the way she'd kept on taking the Pill when they were trying for a baby, and then for the ultimate betrayal with his best friend. Would he understand that she'd loved their unborn baby and hadn't wanted to harm it that day when she'd ignored her obstetrician's advice and gone swimming? Would he understand that, initially, she hadn't been able to bring herself to speak about it?

But now that she'd met him again it was even more difficult to tell him. She couldn't bear to break up their fragile relationship before it had a chance to develop into something stronger. It was like an embryo that required nurturing if it was going to survive. Any kind of harsh treatment would kill it before it had even lived.

'Greg. . .'

'Yes? What's the matter, Lindy? You're so pale.'

He was stroking her cheek with his long, sensitive fingers. He seemed so approachable, now. Did she dare to risk shattering their rapport with her revelations and. . .?

His lips covered hers in a long, sensual kiss. She felt the arousal deep inside her growing as it had on that first night together. The two years rolled away; she was young and innocent again, free of recriminations and obligations, in the arms of the most exciting man she'd ever met.

His hands moved to caress her cheeks, her shoulders, teasing her breasts; she strained against his firm, muscular body, realising that she wanted the ultimate fulfilment of their lovemaking.

His strong arms were lifting her up, carrying her across the carpet.

'We'll be more comfortable in here,' he said, pushing open the door that led into the bedroom.

He undressed her ever so gently, pausing to kiss her burgeoning breasts, sending frissons of sensual pleasure over her body as he explored her skin with his tongue before holding her against him on the bed, his hands caressing her into a state of frenzied desire.

She tightened herself around him as he entered her, the thrill and wonder of their rhythmic union as intense as on that first night together. She cried out as she reached a final, ecstatic climax, and he held her close against him as the sensual waves flooded over her.

She fell asleep in his arms. When she awoke she couldn't remember where she was. It was the ringing of a phone that had wakened her.

'Greg Dalton,' she heard him say sleepily, the phone resting on the pillow against his ear. 'Yes, Sister Sharp, I'm sure you are sorry to wake me but not as sorry as I am.'

She began to wriggle out of his arms but he tightened his grasp as he listened to the night sister.

'Yes, OK. Don't worry. I'll come along now.'

He put the phone down and turned to Lindy, brushing his lips sensually across her cheek before lingering for a few moments on her mouth.

'What's the problem on Nightingale?' she asked as Greg pulled away and got up off the bed.

'Brian Mason disconnected the IV when Sister gave baby Darren the first feed of 5ml glucose and water. She thinks he's becoming dehydrated but Brian refuses to reinsert the IV until I've had a look at him. He says I did the operation so I should have the final say in the matter. James is still tied up with that emergency Caesarean, and Sister doesn't want to bring Brad out from Cragdale.'

Lindy gave a wry grin. 'I don't blame her. Brad wouldn't be in a very good mood if he got dragged back here, complete with hangover, after a night at the banquet.'

He returned to sit down on the edge of the bed,

pulling the fisherman's jersey over his head. She sat up, putting both hands on his chest to smooth down the wool fibres.

'Mmm,' he murmured, pulling her against him. 'We had only a couple of sips of champagne last night but we celebrated in style.' He stood up. 'I'll hurry back. Don't fall asleep again because—'

'Greg, I'm going back to my room.'

A shadow crossed his face. 'Why? I thought—'

'I need to get some more sleep and if I stay here. . .'

He gave a rakish grin and rumpled her hair affectionately. 'If you stay here we'll wear each other out.'

'Something like that,' she said quickly. 'I hope Darren's going to be all right.'

'I'm sure he'll pull through. If he really is dehydrated I'll put him back on the IV. If not, we'll continue the feeds as I ordered before. Brian Mason is a stickler for protocol, apparently. He's just playing safe by calling me along for a second opinion.'

He paused by the door and blew her a kiss. 'I hope you'll still be here when I get back.'

She smiled but didn't reply. It had been so idyllic that she didn't want to shatter his illusions at this stage. Emotionally she felt about him exactly as she had on that first night. But it was impossible to turn the clock back on events. The water that had flowned under the bridge wasn't about to turn back upstream.

One day soon, she promised herself as she pulled on her clothes, she would come clean. But she wanted to be sure that he loved her as much as she now realised she loved him. Being good in bed together was a wonderful experience but it didn't always mean that you were in love with each other. She was sure of her own feelings but she wasn't sure of Greg's. They'd been pretending for so long that it was difficult to realise that the pseudo-affair had turned into a real one. . .or had it? She wished she could get rid of her feelings of uncertainty about the situation.

She went quietly out into the corridor, closing the door gently behind her, hearing the Yale lock click. There was no going back in there now. Greg would be disappointed when he returned but it was better this way.

He didn't phone her the next morning as she'd thought he might. She'd managed to sleep for a couple of hours and then got up and went straight to Nightingale. Brian Mason was checking the monitor on baby Darren.

'Hello, Brian,' Lindy said. 'Darren's back on his IV, I see.'

'Yes, Dr Dalton thought he needed it. The amount he takes by mouth isn't enough to stave off dehydration.'

Lindy sat down beside the cot and smoothed her fingers over the baby's wizened skin. Yes, the intravenous glucose and saline mixture was certainly necessary, but, she decided, checking the monitor, all the other clinical signs were hopeful.

'He didn't seem too pleased when I dragged him out of bed in the early hours,' Brian nodded.

'Shh!' Lindy said as she saw Greg coming through the door. He looked as if he hadn't had time to shave; there was a definite dark stubble on his chin. He was still wearing the fisherman's jersey that reminded her so poignantly of the night they'd spent together, and he looked tired, desperately tired, as if he'd had a disturbed night. . .or, rather, disturb*ing* night, she thought wickedly.

Her heart went out to him and she longed to put her arms around him. At the very least she would have liked to find a comb and run it through the rumpled hair that she'd so recently tangled with her fingers.

'My ears were burning just now,' he said, in the tone that Lindy always recognised as his senior doctor voice. He'd used it on her a few times, and she knew that it was designed to quell any thoughts of insubordination.

'I expect you were discussing the fact that I snapped your head off in the early hours of this morning, Dr Mason.'

'Not at all, sir. I wouldn't have had you called if—'

'It's time you junior doctors learned to take some responsibility. After all, you've had nearly a year in the house, haven't you?'

'One week to go, sir,' Brian replied nervously.

'And then what are your plans?' Greg asked.

'I'm going to join my father's surgery. He's a GP.'

'Will you find that more interesting than working in hospital?'

'It will be different.'

'Certainly will.' Greg turned to look at Lindy. His eyes held a guarded expression as he struggled to remain professional with her.

'And Dr Cash is intending to take a permanent post in the infertility clinic. Let's hope she's successful.'

'I'll second that,' Lindy said quietly as her confidence began once more to ebb away.

She just had to keep her job! Her whole future depended upon it, especially now when her relationship with Greg had taken a turn in the right direction.

Sister Gregson bustled into the room. 'It's time for baby Darren's hourly feed.'

'We'll leave you to it,' Greg said, putting a hand under Lindy's arm and drawing her outside into the corridor.

'I missed you this morning,' he said quietly.

She couldn't control the colour flaming into her cheeks.

He gave her a rakish grin. 'You're blushing.'

'Look, don't embarrass me in front of Ann Gregson, of all people.'

'Oh, I dare say she's had her moments,' he whispered. 'But seriously, I just wanted to warn you that the interview panel will probably give you the third degree next week. I shall be on the panel but I can't help you if you're not able to answer the questions. My advice is to spend as much time as you can this week swotting up the treatment of infertility, and we'll hope for the best. And don't forget to be polite to Sir Jack Hamilton. He's chairing the panel.'

Lindy groaned. 'Oh, God! And I gave him the brush-off last night, didn't I?'

'You certainly did. I hope he forgives you.'

'Dr Dalton, I wonder if I might have a word?' Sister Gregson was holding open the door to the prem unit. 'I think we could increase the fluids by mouth and discontinue the IV. Mr Prestcot hasn't arrived yet so I'd like you to authorise it.'

Greg gave her a charming smile. 'Here we go again,' he muttered under his breath to Lindy. 'Be right with you, Sister.'

During the next few days Lindy realised that Greg was making a valiant effort to be decidedly professional with her. In one way she welcomed this because she had to get herself mentally geared up for the interview for her job, and the fact that Greg would be on the panel was making her apprehensive. She just hoped that she wouldn't make any awful gaffes.

There were one or two evenings as she swotted up her textbooks on infertility when she would have welcomed a diversion, but she reasoned that she ought to be totally prepared for what might be an ordeal, considering that Sir Jack Hamilton was going to chair the panel.

She looked longingly at the phone on the desk in her room. If Greg invited her over for coffee or out for a drink, would she go?

Of course she would!

But the phone remained silent, and she plodded on, forcing herself to cram theories and treatments into her brain. They wouldn't be able to fault her clinical knowledge, but would they think she was temperamentally suitable for the post?

On the morning of the interview Lindy took a great deal of care when she dressed. Nothing had been overlooked. Her nails were neatly manicured, her hair newly shampooed and brushed until it shone. She looked at herself in the mirror. She was wearing her interview suit. She'd bought it two years ago in the States, soon after her miscarriage, and it was definitely a size too large now.

She remembered how her half-sister, Lucy—dear, helpful little blonde, blue-eyed Lucy—had talked her into going shopping with her.

'You need something to boost your morale, Lindy,' she'd said in her mid-Atlantic accent. Lucy never could decide whether she was English or American; she considered that she held allegiance to both countries because she shared her English mother with Lindy and had an American father.

All this had come about because Lindy's mother, Ruth, had left her father when Lindy was three. Then thirty years old, Ruth had fallen in love with a twenty-five-year-old, up-and-coming American artist who had been spending a few months in London while some of his paintings were being exhibited. Lindy vaguely remembered the upheaval at home but it hadn't been too traumatic for her because her Irish grandmother had moved in long before to take care of the household, and life had gone on as usual.

Her mother had been an art teacher, and Lindy had spent most of her time with Grandma before the split. Her father, who had been much older than her mother, settled down into a quiet bachelor existence, distancing himself from the domestic arrangements that his capable mother took care of.

As far as Lindy was concerned, it had been a bonus to belong to two families; the time she'd spent at her mother and stepfather's wooden bungalow by the sea on Cape Cod had been infinitely more exciting than being at home in the conventional semi-detached house in the London suburbs. And then along had come Lucy.

As a child, Lindy had loved playing with her little half-sister, who was five years younger than she. Later on, when the gap in age had seemed to narrow, they had become firm friends who could tell each other secrets knowing that not one word of what they'd said would ever be repeated.

Lucy had often been invited to stay in London by Lindy's father, and had been accepted as part of the extended family. He had never married again, and when he'd died when Lindy was twenty it had been Lucy who'd come over to comfort her and help with the funeral arrangements, just as she had done a couple of years before when Grandma Cash had died.

So, when Lucy had recommended a shopping expedition to put her on her feet and bring her back to the land of the living after her miscarriage, Lindy had decided to put herself in Lucy's capable hands. There had been a cute little boutique at the edge of Provincetown, crammed in between a couple of art galleries, and Lucy had talked Lindy into buying what she called an 'executive suit'.

'You know you're going to be back on the job market again soon, Lindy,' Lucy had told her. 'Use a bit of power-dressing. Look the part of the successful doctor!'

At the time Lindy hadn't even felt that she was a successful human being, and after more than three months of not working in hospital her confidence in her medical skills had been severely eroded, but she'd gone along with the idea to please her half-sister.

She looked now into the mirror at the reflection of the dark grey suit and the long-sleeved white blouse severely buttoned up to the neck. It wasn't her usual image, but it had got her the job here as a house surgeon. Hopefully, she might be able to convince the panel that she was the right candidate for this far more important position.

She pinched the waist in with her fingers and groaned; the suit was positively hanging off her, but maybe they would think she liked it that way. She tilted her chin and flashed a defiant smile. It was the image that counted.

She glanced at her watch. If she walked slowly and breathed deeply, she would arrive in an excellent frame of mind to give a good account of herself. She mustn't be late, but neither must she be too early and give herself exam nerves.

The stone stairs leading from the residents' quarters to the interior of the hospital had never seemed so steep. She paused by the bust of Alexander Fleming.

'Wish me luck,' she whispered as she turned the corner.

'Good morning, Dr Cash.' Sir Jack Hamilton was being coolly polite as he waved a hand towards a large, polished oak carver chair that had been placed in front of the panel of six men seated at the long table in the old refectory of the hospital. 'Do sit down.'

Lindy took a deep breath as she walked across to the awe-inspiring chair. It reminded her of something out of *Mastermind*.

'Good morning, gentlemen,' she said in a firm, clear voice that belied the butterflies flapping about in her tummy.

Out of the corner of her eye she could see Greg seated near the end of the table, flanked by Bradley Prestcot and Simon Delaware. All three looked uncharacteristically serious, and utterly professional. She knew instinctively that she would get no favouritism just because she had friends in high places.

At the other end of the table she recognised a couple of visiting consultants, Raymond Jackson and Vernon Driscoll, both experts in the field of obstetrics and infertility. They were often called in to the Moortown General for interviews and examinations.

Sir Jack Hamilton, in the middle of the panel, was directly in front of her. He cleared his throat, glancing down at his notes before fixing her with a narrow-eyed stare.

'Infertility clinics come in for a lot of criticism, Dr Cash. What would you say to someone who thought it was a waste of resources because the success rate is so low?'

'I would remind them that, even though the latest statistics reveal that only thirty-five per cent of infertile couples seeking help actually conceive as a result of the treatment they undergo, in terms of human satisfaction, they would only have to speak to any of these fortunate couples to realise that being a parent is the most precious experience of their lives.'

The chairman nodded and the corners of his mouth

moved almost into a smile. 'Quite so. Now tell me some of the tests you would perform on an infertile couple.'

This was easy! Lindy systematically elaborated on sperm counts for the man and testing for ovulation— the production of eggs in the woman. When she mentioned endometrial biopsy, which examined the lining of the womb, Bradley Prestcot asked her about the actual procedure. She described how a small pipe was inserted through the cleaned cervix of the womb, usually between the eighteenth and the twenty-eighth day of the menstrual cycle.

Vernon Driscoll now began to question her on procedures in a toneless, typical professional examiner's voice. She could feel her nerves stretched to the limit as she answered questions on testing the Fallopian tubes by laparoscopy.

'We insert a thin telescope into the abdominal cavity through a small hole in the navel,' she began, before going on to describe how a little carbon dioxide gas would have first been passed into the abdomen, to separate the organs and make it easier to get a good view.

The other members of the panel questioned her. There were no trick questions as far as she could make out, but she was glad that she'd spent time revising the theory of infertility because, after the initial straightforward questions, they certainly put her knowledge of some of the more obscure theories to the test.

There was a brief pause, during which she could actually hear the round, railway-station-type clock on the wall behind the panel of men ticking away the seconds. Ye gods, she'd been in here nearly an hour and a half!

The six men were all scribbling systematically; the chairman had passed an ominous-looking sheet of paper to the visiting examiners, who were reading it and nodding their heads. Was that good or bad? She wished someone would say something and put her out of her misery.

At last! Her spirits rose as Greg began to speak in a clear, precise, professional tone. He must have known that she couldn't bear the waiting.

'Dr Cash. . .'

She looked across the room at the man in whose arms she'd spent the night only days ago, willing herself to imagine that he was a stranger.

He asked her to enumerate some of the causes of female infertility. She began with hormonal problems, proceeding on to scarred ovaries, followed by premature menopause. She had been talking for several minutes when the chairman interrupted her.

'Yes, thank you, Dr Cash. I think that's enough about the clinical knowledge required for the job. What I'd like to know is, do you think you have the right temperament for this post?'

She drew in her breath. Now for it! 'I think so,' she said quietly. 'Otherwise I wouldn't be putting myself forward, would I?'

Out of the corner of her eye she saw Greg put his head in his hands and look down at his notes. She mustn't blow it now, even though she considered that it had been a stupid question.

The chairman fixed his beady eyes on her. 'What sort of person do you think we're looking for?'

She hesitated. 'Somebody with integrity; someone who the patients will relate easily to; someone they can confide in and know their secrets won't be revealed.'

Greg was raising his head, a wry smile on his face. Their eyes met, and she couldn't help smiling back. They both knew which patients she'd got that sort of experience from!

Sir Jack cleared his throat again. 'May we all share the joke, Dr Cash?'

'It's not a joke, sir,' Lindy replied evenly. 'It was a shared experience that Dr Dalton and I had with one of our patients. The patient told us a secret which I'm not at liberty to divulge.'

'A shared experience,' the chairman repeated. 'Do you think it's an asset to have a female and a male doctor working harmoniously together as a recognised couple in the infertility clinic? What I'm trying to say is, would you consider that this is welcomed by the patients?'

Lindy hesitated, knowing that Sir Jack was getting at her for the way she'd brushed him off at the banquet. She didn't dare look at Greg. She knew that he would be as tense as she was, waiting for her answer.

'I think the patients find it easier to talk in the relaxed atmosphere they find when medical staff get on well together,' she replied, knowing that it was an ambiguous answer but not wanting to commit herself further. How could she when she didn't know whether she and Greg would ever be able to sort out their differences?

'I see,' the chairman said gravely. 'Would you say that you and Dr Dalton agree on most professional matters?'

She hesitated, again not daring to look at Greg. 'We don't agree as a matter of course. Each medical case is taken on its merit and the facts as they present themselves.'

'But Dr Dalton, as the senior doctor, should be able to overrule your ideas, shouldn't he, Dr Cash?' Sir Jack persisted.

'That would depend,' she said cautiously. 'If I felt I was right and he was wrong I would say so.'

'I'm sure you would,' the chairman replied in a dry

tone. 'Thank you, Dr Cash. We'll let you know our decision this afternoon.'

Oh, God, how would she get through the next few hours? Her legs felt as if they'd turned to jelly as she went out of the door.

'Dr Cash, you're wanted on Nightingale.'

She looked at the student nurse waiting in the corridor.

'Sister Gregson told me to wait here until you came out. One of your mothers has gone into labour and she's asking for you.'

Lindy smiled. 'Thanks, Nurse. Fill me in on the details while we walk up there.'

It was good to be working again. So what if they hadn't liked her in there? So what if she'd blown it? There were other jobs. She would always find work.

And if Greg loved her he wouldn't mind where she worked. And if he didn't she was back where she started a couple of months ago. She could survive without him, but life would never be the same again.

CHAPTER SEVEN

'DR CASH, thank goodness you're here. But then, you told me you would be and I knew you wouldn't let me down.'

Lindy took hold of her patient's hand. Helen Ferguson was producing her first baby at the age of forty-five and she looked petrified.

'You're going to be fine, Helen,' Lindy said. 'Just lie still and I'll see how far on you are.'

As Lindy examined the birth canal she was remembering her patient's long and difficult case history. Helen Ferguson and her husband had been trying for a baby for ten years; during this time she'd suffered four miscarriages. She'd refused to give up, and on this fifth pregnancy she'd reached full term.

When the pregnancy had been fourteen weeks on Lindy had assisted Bradley Prestcot in stitching up the cervix, or neck of the womb, with a Shirodkar suture, which was rather like the drawstring around a purse. This had been necessary because Helen's cervical muscles were too slack.

After the vaginal examination, Lindy checked out the abdomen and reluctantly agreed with the diagnosis that James Dewhirst had written down after the scan when Helen had been admitted. Yes, there was no doubt that the baby was lying firmly in the breech presentation. Instead of the baby's head being engaged, ready to proceed down the birth canal, the little buttocks were waiting to be delivered first.

'Dr Dewhirst took the Shirodkar suture out of the cervix half an hour ago,' said Staff Midwife Jean Smith, leaning over the patient from the other side of the bed. 'The contractions seem to have slowed down since then.'

Lindy nodded. 'Yes. Your baby's going to be some time yet, Helen,' she told her anxious patient. 'Why don't you get up and walk around a bit? It will help to pass the time. Go and have a chat in the day room.'

'Oh, I couldn't!' Helen Ferguson said. 'It was so painful when I came in a couple of hours ago. Are you sure it's not ready to be born?'

'Quite sure,' Lindy said in a sympathetic tone. 'Now come on; a little gentle walk will get things moving again. I'll ask Nurse to bring you a cup of coffee.'

Jean Smith helped Helen into the day room while Lindy checked out Helen's charts with James Dewhirst, who'd just arrived from a session in Outpatients. It appeared that Helen's uterine contractions had been strong on admission but had disappeared after the Shirodkar stitch had been removed. But the most worrying aspect of the case was the breech presentation.

'We've got problems here,' James said quietly. 'A nervous, older, first-time mother after four miscarriages, non-existent contractions and a breech presentation. I've just called Brad but I'm told he's in conference and can only be disturbed for dire emergencies.'

Lindy groaned. 'All the bigwigs are mulling over whether they want me to have a permanent appointment in the infertility clinic.'

'How did the interview go?'

'Don't ask! I was utterly truthful which isn't always a good idea. I suppose I should have sucked up to them a bit more but that's not my style.

'Anyway, to return to our patient's problems, I think we should wait an hour or so, and if the contractions are still weak we should give her intravenous Oxytocin to hurry them along, coupled with an epidural to block out the pain.'

James Dewhirst raised an eyebrow. 'And the breech presentation?'

'I'd like to try to turn the baby round by doing an external cephalic version,' she said evenly.

James frowned. 'Don't you think it would be easier if we did a Caesarean section?'

Lindy hesitated. 'It might come to that, but I'd prefer to try a normal birth. Helen won't feel anything when she's had the epidural.'

'Let me find out what Brad thinks.'

Lindy shrugged. 'I doubt you'll be able to get hold of him, but by all means try. I'll go and have a chat with Helen and try to get her relaxed. Whatever we decide, we don't want her to be worn out with worry.'

'Yes, a natural birth is what I'd really like, Dr Cash,' Helen said a few minutes later as Lindy walked slowly beside her along the corridor outside Nightingale Ward. 'After all, I may not have another baby at my age, and it would be nice to have Mother Nature in on this, rather than a surgical operation. But I'm so scared I—'

'There's no need to be scared. We'll block out the pain and—'

Lindy broke off in mid-sentence. Greg was striding towards her with a grim face.

'Any news?' she asked, almost holding her breath.

'I've been asked to come away from the discussion while they make up their minds. The chairman thought I had a vested interest,' he said quickly and quietly, all in one breath, before turning to look at the pregnant woman. 'Are you our VIP patient?'

Helen preened visibly at the words of the handsome young doctor.

She smiled. 'I hope so. I'm Helen Ferguson; cervical incompetence, fifth pregnancy after four miscarriages, and hoping to be delivered as soon as possible.'

Lindy watched, fascinated, as Greg smiled back, deciding that he could charm the birds from the trees.

'I'm Greg Dalton. Your consultant, Bradley Prestcot, sends his apologies but he's unavoidably delayed. He'll be along as soon as he can. In the meantime he's asked me to take care of you, along with Dr Cash. Do I detect you've had some medical training, Mrs Ferguson? From the way you gave me your case history just now I thought—'

'I was a medical secretary in Leeds for fifteen years,' Helen said. 'I stopped work ten years ago when I was thirty-five so I could start the family, but it just didn't happen. I didn't mention I'd worked in a hospital before because I'm terribly rusty on medical matters now and things have moved on so quickly.'

Greg flashed her another dazzling smile. 'The basics are still there; we won't have to spell it out for you— treat you like a novice, I mean. Would you mind terribly settling yourself in the day room while I confer with Dr Cash about the quickest way of getting your first-born out?'

'Not at all, Dr Dalton,' Helen Ferguson said as she ambled her way back through the day-room door.

Lindy smiled up at Greg. 'Thanks; I'm glad you're here; I was just feeling as if I could do with some help on this one.'

He moved closer to her and put a hand on her arm. 'That's what partnerships are all about.'

'Oh, don't!' she said, turning away. 'What have they been on about down there?'

'I'm not allowed to say,' he replied evenly. 'On clinical theory you're off the hook. But they can't decide whether you're the best partner for me or not.'

'Partner?' she echoed. 'That's a very emotive word.'

He gave a rakish grin. 'They were speaking in a professional way, although it would have helped if you'd told them we made a good partnership, and that we were planning a long-term relationship from which the patients would benefit by having our own experience to draw upon.'

Her pulses raced. 'But that wouldn't have been true,' she said quickly. 'We were only pretending.'

'What about last week? Were we pretending then?'

'You tell me,' she said quickly.

She wished that she could answer that one. Certainly there had been no pretence on her part. She'd been involved in every heart-stopping moment, and, if she was honest, she'd challenged him just now to test out how he really felt. If only he'd been more positive— told her that the pretence was over and the real affair was just starting.

'I wish I knew what was going on inside that pretty little head,' he said huskily.

'Let's get on with the work,' she said quickly, to counteract the frisson of excitement buzzing down her spine. She moved away and walked back into the ward, terribly aware that Greg was close behind, almost touching her. But now wasn't the time to discuss their personal relationship. They had to channel all their energies into solving their patient's problems.

They had a rapid consultation with James Dewhirst, after which Greg said he was inclined to agree with Lindy.

'The patient wants a normal birth. It may be her first and last so let's try to achieve it. And I see no reason why Lindy shouldn't do an external cephalic version if she wants to.'

'Oh, now that you're here, Greg,' she said quickly, 'maybe you should do it.'

Greg was adamant. 'I'd like to see what you can do, Dr Cash,' he said in an ultra-professional voice. 'You were happy to do it on your own. What's the difference now that I'm breathing down your neck?'

'Exactly! You've hit the nail on the head. You'll be breathing down my neck and making me nervous.'

'I'll try not to; if you're in any difficulty I'll take over. Trust me.'

Their eyes met. 'Oh, I do,' she said evenly. 'In most things.'

A glimmer of a smile crossed his lips. 'If we're all agreed then, I'll call up the anaesthetist to come and do the epidural.'

Helen Ferguson lay very still as the effects of the epidural anaesthetic began to be felt. Lindy put her hands on her patient's abdomen, feeling for the outline of the precious baby. She felt decidedly agitated. There was so much at stake. She didn't want to harm this long-awaited child. And Greg's eyes on her hands were making her nervous. It wasn't as if she hadn't performed a cephalic version before. This was probably her fourth or fifth, but it felt like her first as she moved her fingers over the outline of the baby's buttocks.

'Just relax, Helen; I won't hurt you.'

'I can't feel a thing below the waist, Dr Cash,' the patient said.

'That's good,' Lindy said, concentrating on the position of the baby in its mother's uterus.

Firmly she moved the baby's head towards its feet until the head felt as if it was over the edge of Helen's pelvis. She looked up at the Oxytocin IV, steadily dripping its speeding-up drug. She was hoping that the contractions would increase before the baby tried to move back into its breech presentation, as so often happened.

'Babies can be very stubborn,' she whispered to Greg. 'I hope this one will take the message and decide I know what's best for it.'

Greg smiled. 'That was a good manouevre, Doctor. I wouldn't try to get out of that if I were Helen's baby.'

He looked down at the patient. 'What are you going to call your baby, Helen?'

The patient smiled. 'From the various scans, they've told me it's a boy, so I'll call him Michael after my father. I'm an only child, and his first, long-awaited grandson is going to be spoilt rotten!'

'You can say that again,' said a masculine voice as Helen's husband, gowned and masked, arrived through the door.

'Robert! Come and hold my hand,' Helen called out from the delivery table. 'I didn't think you were going to make it. What kept you?'

'I asked the pilot but he couldn't make the plane go any faster,' Robert Ferguson replied. 'You might have waited until I got back from the Far East before you went into labour, Helen.'

Despite the broad smile and the attempt at a joke, Lindy could see that Robert Ferguson was as nervous as his wife had been.

'Sit down here, Mr Ferguson,' she said gently, pulling out a chair. 'Is there anything we can get you—tea, coffee. . .?'

'A large whisky?' he suggested, leaning over his wife and kissing her gently on the cheek.

'We're clean out of whisky,' Greg said as a nurse slotted him into a clean gown. 'I'd settle for coffee if I were you.'

The contractions began to increase in length and intensity. Lindy's hand on the outside of the pelvic brim felt the baby move down to engage its head in the bony entrance to the birth canal.

'Well done, Michael!' she said under her breath as Greg stationed himself at the foot of the table, his hands ready to guide the baby out.

The entire birth lasted a matter of minutes as the Oxytocin took effect; the uterine muscles pushed out the head, followed by the shoulders and then the body of the already much loved baby.

'Michael's got a loud voice!' Greg said, smiling broadly as he placed the still-slippery infant in his mother's arms.

'He's wonderful! Just perfect. Doesn't he look like Robert with a hangover? Oh, thank you so much!'

The tears streamed down Helen Ferguson's face as she admired the miracle bundle in her arms.

'You were wonderful too,' Greg said, patting the proud mother's arm. 'A model patient. I'll be happy to deliver the next one.'

'Don't think I could stand the strain!' the proud father said. 'Now, about that drink. I happen to have brought a couple of bottles of champagne from the Duty-Free in Singapore airport, so if any of the staff would care to join me. . .'

'We'd love to, Mr Ferguson,' Lindy put in quickly, 'but we're not allowed to drink on duty. But you go ahead. We'll find you a glass and. . .'

'I'll leave one of the bottles for you to drink later,' Robert said.

After Sister Gregson had arrived to take charge of the new baby, Lindy told Greg that she was going to go down to the porters' lodge to see if there was a message for her.

'They must have come to a conclusion by now,' she said, feeling a rush of the anxiety that she'd been holding back during Helen's delivery.

'I'll come with you,' Greg said quickly, stripping off his gown and handing it to one of the nurses.

As she walked beside him down the long corridor outside Nightingale Lindy could feel the tension increasing.

'I think I'm even more nervous than I was before the interview,' she told him, making an attempt at a forced laugh and failing miserably.

'You're not the only one,' he said, his voice breathy with emotion.

She looked up at him. 'Does it matter so much to you? It's not your future that's at stake.'

He stopped in the corridor and took both her hands in his. 'Isn't it?' he said quietly.

She looked up into his eyes, feeling that her heart would stop beating. This had to be real, this feeling of closeness. Greg wasn't pretending now.

'Lindy! Greg! I've got a message for you.'

She took her hands away and turned to see Bradley Prestcot hurrying towards them.

'I'm on my way to see Helen Ferguson,' he said. 'How's she doing?'

Greg filled Brad in on the details, while Lindy waited with baited breath.

'You said you had a message for me, Brad,' she prompted.

'Oh, yes, almost forgot.'

Lindy held her breath. She was sure that Brad hadn't forgotten; he was just keeping her in suspense.

'Congratulations! Sir Jack is drafting out the contract with his secretary right now.'

'Oh, thank God!' Lindy ran a hand over her face and Greg put out his arm to steady her as she swayed. 'I was beginning to think that. . .well, I thought maybe Sir Jack would think I was too outspoken.'

'As a matter of fact, Lindy,' Brad said, with a wry grin, 'Sir Jack had nothing but praise for you—said he admired women who spoke their minds.'

'Well, he had a funny way of showing it down there in the interview,' Lindy said, feeling weak with relief. 'He was positively glaring at me most of the time.'

'Come on, I'm going to take you off duty. You've had enough for one day,' Greg said, putting a hand under her arm.

'Yes, I think you should take good care of your junior partner, Greg,' Brad said as he went off towards Nightingale.

Lindy smiled as they walked down the steps to the residents' quarters. Greg's junior partner! Was that what she wanted to be? It would do for a start, and later, when they sorted out their differences, maybe. . .

'Hey, what's so funny?' he asked as they reached the foot of the stairs.

She shook her head. 'Can't tell you yet. Got to work something out first.'

'Got to celebrate before we do anything else!' He put his hands on the sides of her arms, holding her in a firm grip as he bent his head towards her. 'Come home with me, Lindy, to the pink house. There's champagne cooling in the fridge and I'll organise a party to celebrate your success.'

She hesitated. The last thing she needed was a crowd of medics, talking shop and jollying each other along. 'Who will you invite?'

He grinned. 'Just you.'

Her spirits soared. 'Well, then, I accept your invitation.'

'Can you be ready in ten minutes, Lindy?'

'Give me half an hour.' She wanted to look her best.

She showered and slipped into the camel-coloured linen trousers she'd bought from the Good As New shop a couple of days before. They would have been far too expensive for her if she'd bought them new.

Teaming them with her favourite, much worn, well-washed green silk shirt, she felt confident.

As she pulled on her leather sandals a tingle of excitement ran through her at the prospect of the evening ahead. If they made love and she felt that he was totally committed to her, would she now dare to tell him about the baby she'd lost. . .his baby? What would his reaction be if she did? Why didn't she just tell him she'd miscarried and leave out the guilt she continually felt at knowing that she might have saved the baby if she'd taken her obstetrician's advice? Would it remind him too much of how his ex-wife had cheated him out of fatherhood?

There was a knock on the door. She took a deep breath. No turning back, she thought. Just tell him! If she could face those difficult men on the panel she could face just one man who was, at the very least, physically attracted to her.

His eyes swept over her appraisingly. 'Worth waiting for,' he said, taking hold of her hand. 'Come on, let's not waste any more time.'

She did her own appraisal of him as they walked out to the car—well-pressed jeans and cotton shirt open at the collar, revealing dark hairs reaching to the hollow at the base of his neck.

The journey over to Cragdale took only a few minutes.

'It's so convenient having a house here,' Greg said, jumping out of the car as soon as he'd pulled into the driveway of the pink house. He went round and opened the passenger door.

Lindy climbed out and breathed in the fresh air.

'Mmm, it may be only a few minutes from Moortown but it seems a million miles away in reality. It's like being in the middle of the countryside.'

Greg laughed. 'We are in the middle of the countryside. We've got the whole spread of the Yorkshire Dales all around us. It's just that Moortown had the audacity to plonk itself in the middle and keep on spreading its tentacles.'

Lindy looked around her at the cottage garden that threatened to revert to its natural state on the wild hillside. Late flowering daffodils and primroses jockeyed for position with the daisies in the long grass under the budding lilac and laburnum trees.

'It's very picturesque,' Lindy said.

Greg laughed. 'Which is your way of saying I'm not much of a gardener. My excuse is I haven't got much spare time outside hospital. When I've tamed you I'll turn my attention to the garden.'

'No chance! You'd better get yourself a gardener,' she said, watching him unlock the thick oak door, which creaked on its hinges as it swung open.

Having got used to the bright pink of the outside, she was surprised by the dark colours of the interior. Oak panelling in the diminutive hall seemed overgrand for the size of the cottage. Her feet resounded on the tiled floor as she followed Greg into the decidedly unfitted kitchen.

'The cottage is about a hundred years old and, as you can see, I haven't changed anything since I moved in. I've bought the essentials like a bed, a sofa, a carpet for the sitting room and so on. It all takes time, which I haven't got.

'I'm not much of a home-maker. Take after my parents, I suppose. They lived in rented accommodation all their married lives and never added to or changed anything in the houses they were in. They were both lecturers, more interested in the piles of books gathering dust than the colour of the curtains.'

'It lacks a woman's touch,' Lindy said lightly.

He turned round from opening the fridge, a bottle of champagne in his hand.

'Are you offering, Lindy?'

'You'd never be able to afford me,' she quipped.

He gave her a rakish grin. 'Have some champagne and then we'll negotiate the terms and conditions.' He removed the cork and poured out a couple of glasses. 'To our new partnership.'

Lindy raised her glass and their eyes met.

'Congratulations, Lindy,' he said huskily. 'You batted very well this morning.'

He put down his glass and pulled her towards him.

'Careful, you'll spill my—'

Firmly he removed her glass and put it down on the wooden kitchen table, tightening his arms around her.

'I need some help with the decor in the bedroom. Let's negotiate the terms up there. I'll carry the bottle if you take the glasses.'

She didn't protest. She wanted to make love just as much as he did. She'd been longing for the feel of his arms around her for nearly a week now.

Lindy giggled as their feet clattered on the carpetless stairs. 'There's so much work to be done in this house. My fee is going to be astronomically high. Like I said, you'll never be able to afford me.'

'Couldn't I pay you back in kind?' he said, leading the way into the bedroom.

It was a bright, airy room—easily the largest room in the house. Lindy carried her champagne glass over to the window that faced south-west. The April sun was beginning to dip down behind the fells at the other side of the valley. Greg came up behind her, putting his hands around her shoulders before lowering them to cover her breasts. She could feel the passion rising inside her as they stood bathed in the warm rays of the setting sun, looking out across the valley.

'It's so idyllic here,' she whispered, half to herself.

'So will you take the job?' he murmured into her hair.

'Depends on the terms of the contract,' she said, wriggling free from his arms to turn around and face him.

'Come to bed and we'll discuss it.'

He took both her hands and led her over to the wide four-poster. She sensed his urgency matching her own as he undressed her, slowly. He was trying so desperately not to rush things, but she knew that she herself couldn't hold out for long. The tension was overwhelming as she unbuttoned his shirt, exposing the broad muscles of his dark, hairy chest.

The bed was still crumpled, bachelor-style, from the last time he'd slept in it. He pulled her onto the sheet beside him, covering her body with his own, one hand tantalising her breasts while the other caressed the inner thighs. She could feel the warm, moist rush of excitement that flooded the cleft between her thighs. The tormenting suspense was mounting as she moulded herself against him, resenting even the skin that separated them.

She moaned as she felt his hard manhood pressed against her; she wanted him to take her immediately, without any more foreplay; she was utterly impatient to be joined with him in an erotic, satisfying fusion. His caresses continued to drive her on into a wild state of total abandon before he plunged inside her with an urgency born of frenzied desire.

They climaxed together, both released from the incredible tension that had been building up. Lindy lay still, wanting to remain part of Greg for as long as she could.

'I didn't mean to take you so quickly,' he murmured.

'You didn't take me,' Lindy whispered back. 'We took each other. And I couldn't have waited a moment longer.'

He smiled and reached out a hand to pour some more champagne into their glasses.

She took a sip. This was the point when she'd hoped that he would tell her he loved her. She looked up at the crimson silk canopy and wondered if she dared tell him how she felt about him. She pulled the sheet up. Better wait; better not risk frightening him off if he wasn't ready for commitment. He'd told her that after his wife's deception he'd never wanted to trust another woman as long as he lived. Better keep it light. Give him time to recover and learn to trust again.

'I love the bed,' she told him, putting all her emotion into praising the inanimate object. 'You certainly didn't stint on the fabric or the quality. Where on earth did you find it?'

'I had it made. It's only just been delivered. Before that I was sleeping on a camp-bed. I've been waiting for an occasion to christen it.'

'It's so. . .'

'Romantic?' he suggested.

She nodded, suddenly too full for words.

His arms tightened around her, his hands caressing her body, until she felt herself responding again with a passion equal to his. This time their lovemaking was slow, sensual and infinitely more satisfying.

Afterwards she lay, utterly spent, in his arms, thinking that she had never been so happy in the whole of her life.

'Let's drink to the christening of the bed,' he said, clinking his glass against hers.

'Not christening,' she said quickly. 'Babies are christened. Beds are—'

'Beds are for making love in,' he cut in. 'There's no
need to look so serious. I was only joking about the
christening.'

She swallowed. 'I know.'

Should she tell him now about the baby that would
have been christened if it had lived?

'You've got that strange expression on your face
again,' he said quietly. 'As if you're worrying about
something. Look, cheer up. It's a day for celebration.
You've got the job you wanted on your own merit. You
were excellent this morning. I was so proud of you.'

She took a sip of champagne. 'Were you? I thought
you looked worried most of the time.'

'Well, I must admit I was afraid you'd give the wrong
impression, make the panel think we were still fighting
with each other, unable to agree on anything. And
after all our efforts to make it look as if we were
romantically involved.'

She stiffened. 'When we weren't,' she said in a
subdued voice.

'No, we weren't, but we fooled everybody.' She
couldn't help thinking that it was Greg who'd fooled
everybody. . .even her.

CHAPTER EIGHT

'It's Sara's wedding on Saturday, isn't it?' Greg said, poking his head around the door of Lindy's consulting room at the beginning of a Thursday morning out-patient session. 'I've sent my apologies to Sara's parents. It's going to be impossible to get away; all Brad and Sara's colleagues want to be in on the act. The hospital needs some senior staff to stay behind so I volunteered.'

'Very noble of you,' she said, keeping her eyes on the case notes in front of her.

He took a step inside the room and leaned against the door. 'I thought I'd tell you now in case you were relying on a lift up to the Lakes with me.'

She looked up from the notes she was pretending to study. She didn't like the words 'relying on'. Since he'd made it perfectly clear that very little had changed in their relationship she'd decided never to rely on him again.

'I'm going to drive myself up there,' she said evenly. 'I do have a car, you know, even though it's only an old banger.'

'Lindy. . .?' He took a couple of steps towards her desk.

She felt the inevitable charismatic pull that he exerted over her. How she longed to feel his arms around her again, but how could she trust him? Hadn't he made it perfectly plain that their relationship was all a light-hearted game with him? He hadn't changed one bit since that one-night stand when he'd first charmed his way into her bed.

'Lindy,' he began again, draping his long frame over the side of her desk, 'what did I say that made you want to leave my house so quickly the other evening? Phoning for a cab like that when I thought—'

'When you thought I would stay the night?' she said quietly.

'As a matter of fact I did. There was no reason for you to run away like that.'

'I wasn't running away, as you call it,' she said firmly. 'I wanted to get back to hospital, to my own room. I needed time to think.'

'About what?'

'Your first patients are here,' Rona Phillips announced, pushing open the door. She smiled up at Greg. 'Good morning, Dr Dalton. I've prepared the treatment room for the IVF as you asked. Is there anything else I can do for you?'

'No, thank you, Staff Nurse,' Greg replied quickly.

Only Lindy sensed the exasperation that he was masking under his polite tone as he stood up and left the room.

'I didn't break anything up, did I?' Rona asked. 'I would have knocked if I'd known he was in here. I mean—'

'Oh, don't be silly,' Lindy said irritably. 'Bring our first patients in, please.'

'Yes, *Doctor*,' Rona said, stressing the word.

Lindy drew in her breath as she waited. She mustn't take her frustration out on Rona, but she found it so hard that she and Greg were continually the focus of attention. That was one reason she was glad he wasn't going to be at Sara's wedding. They would have had to withstand jokes about who was going to be the next, and she couldn't take any more of those at the moment.

The first patients, Donna and David Powel, looked

nervous when Rona brought them into Lindy's consulting room.

'Do sit down, and don't look so worried,' Lindy said, putting on a bright smile. 'We'll take good care of you this morning.'

'Just explain again, Doctor, what's actually going to happen,' Donna Powel said quietly.

'Well, as you probably know, Donna, IVF stands for in vitro fertilisation, which literally means fertilisation in glassware. Some people still call it making a test-tube baby. Actually we hardly ever mix the sperm and the eggs on glass dishes, much less in test-tubes, because, as we all know, glass is so difficult to clean. My grandma used to give me extra pocket money to clean the windows at home, and they were always so smeared that you could hardly see out of them. Luckily, Gran was very short-sighted so she used to pay me anyway.'

Donna laughed. 'I have the same problem in our flat. I lean out of the windows squirting this so-called "magic" liquid, and David says they look worse than before.'

Lindy smiled. 'So that's one reason we don't use glass test-tubes. Small plastic dishes are excellent for one time only, and then we throw them away.'

Lindy could see the couple relaxing back against their chairs as they listened. She'd deliberately started on the easy bit; now she had to explain the procedures that they would have to undergo.

'This morning Dave is going to provide us with the sperm,' Lindy said, still smiling reassuringly. 'Don't worry,' she added quickly as a sheepish look crossed his face. 'We know you might find it hard in hospital, so we've got a special bedroom with every possible kind of sexy stimulus imaginable. You can ask for

anything you fancy—apart from one of the nurses
that is.'

David laughed. 'Pity about that. You were beginning
to get me excited, Doctor.'

Lindy smiled. 'You can take as long as you like,
David, and nobody will come in to hassle you. Just
produce the magic potion in your own good time.'

His wife patted his hand. 'You've got the easy bit.
I'm the one who's going to be stretched out on the
operating table while they go painfully searching
for eggs.'

'It's not painful,' Lindy said quickly. 'You've been
taking your clomiphene drugs since your period,
haven't you, Donna? That means your ovaries will
have been stimulated into producing several eggs, and
today is exactly the right time for collecting them. I'm
a dab hand at collecting eggs, by the way. I spent a
few months on a friend's farm helping with the hens,
and every morning it was my job to search the
nesting boxes.'

Donna and David laughed together.

'Are you planning on searching Donna's nesting box,
Doctor?' David asked, with a grin.

Lindy smiled. 'Something like that. It's the same
principle. What we're going to do is take you into the
treatment room, give you a local anaesthetic in and
around the birth canal to remove the sensations, and
then you won't feel a thing. I'll explain what's happening as we go along. Now, do you feel any easier
about it?'

Donna nodded. 'You'll be there, won't you,
Doctor?'

'Of course I will, and you'll have Dr Dalton as well.'

'He's gorgeous! I don't mind him being around,'
Donna said.

'I only hope I can come up with the necessary

ingredients for making this baby,' David said, with a wry look. 'I mean I'm not in the right mood for working myself up this morning.'

'Just think of the first night of our honeymoon and you'll be all right,' Donna said, with a suggestive smile. 'Imagine the waves crashing on the shore outside our hotel in Hawaii, that huge king-size bed with the—'

'OK, OK, that'll do,' David broke in. 'Just lock me up and let me get on with it.'

Minutes later Lindy and Rona were helping Donna onto the treatment-room table. Greg came in and chatted for a few minutes with their patient to put her at ease before he gave her the local anaesthetic.

'It's all gone numb, Doctor,' Donna said.

'Good,' Greg said. 'You won't feel anything, but you'll be able to see what's going on if you watch that ultrasound screen.'

He stepped back so that Lindy could insert a thin ultrasound probe into the patient's vagina. As she moved it higher towards the womb they could see a picture of the ovaries shown clearly on the screen.

'Hold it right there, Lindy,' Greg said as he carefully inserted a special needle through the top of the vagina and with the help of the ultrasound guided it into an ovary. Locating the follicle or capsule surrounding an egg, he siphoned the egg out through the needle; still watching the screen, he searched for another one.

After a few minutes Greg announced that he had removed four eggs from Donna's ovaries.

'Does that mean I'm going to have quads?' she asked incredulously.

Greg shook his head. 'This is only the beginning of the process. We've got to get the eggs fertilized by your husband's sperm first. In a couple of days we'll check to see how many embryos—or potential babies—we've got in our plastic dishes. It's unlikely that they'll all four become viable. Anyway, we do try to limit the number of embryos we put back into the womb nowadays so that we don't create too many multiple births. I mean, how would you feel about having twins?'

'I'd be delighted. Dave and I always wanted a big family,' Donna replied without hesitation.

'Triplets?' Lindy queried.

'Fine!'

'Quads?' Greg asked.

Donna hesitated, pulling a wry face. 'Well, I'm not so sure about quads.'

Greg smiled. 'Don't worry; we won't plant quads on you,' he said as he carefully handed the precious container of eggs to Dr Bill Sutcliffe, the embryologist who was going to examine them in the infertility section of the hospital pathology department.

Bill Sutcliffe always insisted on transporting the eggs himself on their short journey to the path lab. He was an intense but likeable thirty-something man and Lindy had found him a valuable member of the team.

He'd come into the treatment room just minutes before the eggs were removed and waited quietly at the back, as if reluctant to interfere. But, once the eggs were in his possession, Lindy noticed that he became totally possessive about them and took his important work very seriously indeed.

'We'd like you to come back in two days' time, Donna,' Greg said. 'To be on the safe side, give us a call in the morning so that we can let you know if the embryos are ready to be implanted. All being well, we should be able to transfer some of them back into your womb in the afternoon. It's a fairly simple process, you won't need an anaesthetic and you'll be able to go home soon afterwards.'

'But it will be the Easter Weekend!' Donna said, sitting up on the table.

'I know,' Greg said. 'We're open all hours in this place. Once the embryos are ready they need to be transferred or they won't survive. Unless you want me to freeze them, of course?'

'Ooh, no! Let's get on with it.'

'Only joking, Donna,' Greg said. 'Hope to see you on Saturday, then. Dr Cash will be at a wedding but Staff Nurse Phillips will stay and help me, won't you?'

Rona smiled. Of course she would.

Lindy didn't see Greg again until she was struggling to lift a suitcase into the back of her car on Friday evening. He was walking out to his car, looking relaxed in jeans and his old fisherman's sweater.

'Here, let me do that.'

She stood back as he hoisted her suitcase into the boot of the car.

'Are you leaving right now?' he asked.

'This very minute.' She looked up at him, loving the way his mouth was curving into a languid smile.

'Come out to the pink house first,' he said, his voice deep with what she'd come to recognise as his hungry, husky tone.

She felt a quiver of sensual sensation running down her spine, knowing instinctively that he wanted her, right there and then. The raw need was blatant in his dark, expressive eyes. She also knew that she wanted him.

'I'll give you supper and then—'

'Sorry, Greg, I'm going to stay with a friend. She's going to give me supper when I arrive.'

She tried to keep her tone light, not wanting him to know how much she would prefer to be climbing into his car, being driven over to his house for a wonderful night in that romantic four-poster bed.

He took hold of her, very gently, as he bent his head to kiss her slowly, languidly, his lips bringing back memories of all the other times when they'd been together. Oh, God! If only she didn't have to go all the way to the Lake District, she thought.

She stepped back. 'See you on Monday,' she said breezily.

'Drive carefully.' He was already walking over to his car.

She was still fiddling with the ignition key as he drove past and waved.

Several miles outside Moortown Lindy hit the motorway and followed it until she came to the exit for Windermere. Josie's farm was in a small hamlet high in the hills above the lake, and Lindy usually found it by instinct.

The first time she'd been there had been when she was in her early teens, she remembered as she negotiated the rough, narrow road that led out of the Windermere valley. Josephine White, although a year older than Lindy, had been her best friend at boarding-school when she had given her a pressing invitation to go and stay on the family farm for a week in the Easter holidays.

Josie and her widowed father Sam had met her at the station and driven her up this rickety track. They'd been firm friends ever since, and it had been Josie's farm that had seemed like home when Lindy had returned from the States feeling so weak after the miscarriage, and not having a clue as to what she was going to do next.

Josie had kept her busy, teaching her how to milk the cows and feed the hens; she'd tramped over the mountains in all weathers, and little by little, immersed in the outdoor life, as the months had rolled by Lindy had got strong again.

She'd only intended to stay a few weeks, she remembered, but in the end she'd been there through the autumn and right through the winter. As the first snowdrops had started to peep through the snow she'd decided that it was time to get her act together and face the world again. She'd started applying for jobs and been accepted at Moortown General last April.

A whole year ago, she thought as she drove towards the open farm gates. And in that time she'd only managed to get back here a couple of times. So, as soon as she'd heard that Sara's wedding was to be in the Lake District, she'd phoned Josie.

'Lindy!' Josie came running out of the kitchen door as soon as Lindy's tyres ground to a halt in the muddy farmyard. 'Oh, it's so good to see you again. Did you have a good journey? How are you? You're looking thin; been working too hard, I shouldn't wonder. Come inside. The kettle's on the boil.'

Lindy smiled. The kettle was always on the boil in this cosy kitchen. The huge, blackened kettle was placed permanently at the edge of the fire that smouldered on, winter and summer alike.

Sam White, beginning to look his age at almost seventy, got up from his armchair by the fire to give Lindy a warm welcome, telling her that she didn't come to see them often enough.

'I always think of you as the second daughter I might have had if my dear wife hadn't passed on when Josie was born,' he said fondly.

They ate home-made cheese-and-onion pie with baked potatoes and chives, sitting at the scrubbed wooden table. The huge teapot was replenished several times as they caught up with each other's news.

After Sam had gone to bed Josie began questioning

Lindy about life in hospital. Lindy was deliberately evasive. She hadn't been able to bring herself to tell Josie that she'd met Greg again. There was no reason why she should. It would only open up the wounds that she'd tried to heal when she'd spent those months here on the farm.

She was very fond of Josie but knew that she would try to impose her own ideas on the situation, and Lindy wanted to be able to make up her own mind.

She looked up at the grandfather clock and saw that it was past midnight.

'Better get my beauty sleep,' she said, standing up. 'I mustn't be late at the church in the morning.'

'Will he be there, Lindy?' Josie asked quietly.

'Who?'

'Oh, come on, Lindy! It's obvious you've met somebody at the hospital. It stands out a mile. All those half-finished sentences, being dead cagey about the staff in the department you're working in, changing the subject and—'

'OK, OK,' Lindy said. 'Yes, I've met somebody, but I don't want to talk about him at the moment.'

As she looked at Josie's small, intense face with its perceptive expression, framed by the short, dark, slightly wavy hair, she remembered how Josie had been adamant that she must never see Greg again. Josie had told her that Greg was the source of all her misery and that she must avoid him at all costs. In the months that Lindy had lived here on the farm Greg had become the villain of the piece to both of them. That was how she'd thought of him until she'd met him once more and he'd turned her world upside down again.

'I suppose you could say I'm in love,' Lindy said carefully. 'But it's not all plain sailing. There are so many problems that need resolving. Look, Josie, you'll be one of the first to know if we ever manage to sort out our differences but, for the moment, don't ask any more questions.'

Josie smiled. 'You're being very mysterious. Just answer me one question and then I promise not to mention it again until you do. Is he married?'

'No, he's not.'

'Well, then?' Josie spread out her hands. 'What's holding you back? Sorry! I promised no more questions. Subject closed. You look dead on your feet. Goodnight; sleep well; pleasant dreams.'

Lindy's dreams were anything but pleasant as she tossed and turned in the narrow bed by the window that looked out over the rugged Lakeland fells. She was in the same little room that she always slept in at the farm, but tonight sleep eluded her for a long time, and when it came she found herself running around in circles during her dreams. She was in hospital, trying to find Greg; every time she caught up with him he moved away from her; she was trying to run and her legs wouldn't move. . .

'There's someone on the phone downstairs, Lindy.'

She opened her eyes to see Josie standing by her bed.

'Sorry?' She tried to focus her eyes. The morning sun was streaming through the curtains that Josie was opening.

'There's someone on the phone for you.'

Lindy pulled on her dressing gown and went down the stairs.

'Sara! What's the blushing bride doing phoning me on her wedding day?' Lindy said as soon as she recognised her friend's voice.

'Sorry to waken you so early, Lindy. Believe it or not I couldn't sleep; so many last-minute arrangements on my mind. Mum's driving me mad! Anyone would think it was a royal wedding. She's ordered far too many wedding cars and most people are coming in their own. So I wondered if I could persuade you to arrive in one of these posh limos?'

Lindy smiled. 'Are you sure it's not because you don't want my old Mini parked outside the church?'

Sara laughed. 'You've rumbled me! No, seriously, Lindy, I've got to find guests willing to be driven over in style, and you know what our crowd are like. But, you being on your own today, I thought. . .'

'Love to. Thanks a lot. And Sara, good luck!'

'I'm going to need it. Mum doesn't entirely approve of me being three months pregnant at my wedding. She's had the dressmaker unpick my dress and redesign it. It's now got a sort of jacket effect around the waist. I must go; see you in church. Bye.'

Lindy had a leisurely bath and put on trousers and a T-shirt before going downstairs for eggs and bacon in the kitchen. Josie and her father went off to check on the two young farm-hands who came up from Windermere each day, while Lindy cleared the table and washed up.

Back in her room she began to get ready for the wedding. Her suit was olive-green linen. She'd bought it last year to go to the wedding of one of her friends in London and had hardly worn it since, but, being linen, it had creased badly in the case. If only she'd remembered to hang it out last night, but it had been so late and she'd been so tired.

There was an ironing-board in the laundry room to one side of the kitchen. She plugged in the iron and gave the suit a quick going over. As she put it over her arm she heard the crunching of tyres outside.

Ye gods! Through the window she could see a large black limousine standing in the farmyard, a peaked-capped chauffeur talking to Josie.

'I think Lindy's ready,' Josie was saying. 'Lindy! Your carriage awaits!'

Five minutes later she was sitting in the back of the car, hastily applying her make-up as the car purred over the road.

The view from the car window, when she'd finished her make-up, was exhilarating. In the valley below she could see the lake stretched out, the numerous boats looking like toys as they skimmed the sunlit surface. It was a perfect day for a wedding.

And a perfect setting too, she thought as she climbed out of the limo in front of the ivy-covered grey stone church. A stream ran down the side of the churchyard, making its way through the little valley that led to the lake.

The church was almost full. Lindy found herself a place near the back, at the end of one of the few remaining empty pews. In front she recognised many of her colleagues. Hannah and Simon arrived and asked if they could join her.

'Greg stayed behind to hold the fort, I hear,' Hannah said as she sat down next to Lindy.

'Yes, he's got to do an IVF implant today and. . .'

Her voice trailed away; someone was touching her shoulder.

'Room for one more?'

'Greg! Talk of the devil,' Lindy said. 'I thought—'

'Well, have you got room for me there or not?'

Hannah smiled as she moved to one side so that Greg could sit next to Lindy.

'How did you manage to get away? I was just telling Hannah about the IVF,' Lindy said breathlessly.

'We checked out the cultured eggs early this morning and they weren't ready to be implanted. They need another twenty-four hours before we can make a decision about them. So, the hospital was quiet and I thought I'd nip up here for the wedding. It only took me an hour so if I'm needed they can bleep me on the mobile.'

The organist broke off the quiet background music and struck up the opening chords of the 'Bridal March'. It was all so traditional. Lindy had been to lots of weddings but she was always moved when the bride came down the aisle.

Sara looked radiant; the white satin dress fitted her perfectly, and the extra folds around the waist didn't look at all out of place.

As the bridal procession stopped in front of the altar Lindy felt Greg's hand closing over hers. The touch of his fingers sent a shiver of sensual excitement running through her. There was a lump in her throat as she glanced sideways. Oh, God, he looked so handsome in his dark suit!

At that precise moment she knew that she could forgive him anything; did it matter what he'd put her through? But would he forgive her for keeping her secret to herself? Oh, she'd give anything to be standing at the altar with him!

As if in a dream she could hear the vicar asking Sara if she would take Brad to be her wedded husband.

'To have and to hold from this day forward, for better for worse. . .'

She put her other hand—the one that Greg wasn't holding—up to her face and brushed away the tiny tear that was threatening to trickle down her check.

Greg's fingers tightened around hers. 'Are you always like this at weddings?' he whispered.

'Always,' she whispered back. But more especially today.

By the time the organist was playing Mendelssohn's 'Wedding March' she'd got a grip on herself. She didn't want to go out into the bright April sunlight with tears streaming down her face.

Greg was still holding her hand as they went out into the churchyard, and he only released it when she dipped into her handbag to pull out a box of confetti.

'Doesn't Sara look beautiful?' Lindy commented.

'Brides always do,' Greg said quietly. 'It must be the prospect of marriage. It makes them look radiant. We ought to try it.'

She turned to stare at him, her pulses racing.

'Was that a proposal?'

'That's an old-fashioned word. I thought people just had a mutual agreement these days.'

'Marriage is an old-fashioned institution but it seems to work. . .for some people,' Lindy said, her voice unexpectedly cracking as she tried to quell the emotional upheaval churning away inside her.

He was smiling down at her. 'So what do you say we give it a whirl?'

They were standing on the edge of the crowd. Photographs were being taken.

'Lindy! Greg! Come and join in the Moortown General photograph,' Brad called.

'I need an answer, Lindy,' Greg said as he took her hand and led her towards the bridal group.

'Stand here with your lady, sir,' said the photographer. 'We need a good-looking couple near the front.'

'So I wonder whose wedding we'll be going to next?' Sara teased knowingly as the grouping was broken up to make way for the distant relatives.

Lindy smiled back but remained silent.

'It's like an infectious disease, very catching,' Brad said, but his bride disagreed.

'Trust you to find a medical term for it! It feels OK so far, even if we did jump the gun. You're all invited back next spring for the christening.'

'Sara!' remonstrated the bride's mother primly, but the radiant bride continued to smile as if she hadn't got a care in the world.

The reception in the church hall was an elaborate affair. Local caterers had been called in to provide a three-course lunch for over a hundred people. Long trestle-tables covered in starched white linen tablecloths filled the room. Each place-setting had a card with the name of the person intended to sit there. Greg had a quiet word with one of the waitresses and got himself a place next to Lindy.

'Still waiting for my answer,' he whispered as they started on the salmon mousse.

She paused with the fork halfway to her mouth. 'Maybe you could rephrase the question? I'm not sure I like the idea of giving it a whirl. It sounds more like asking me for a dance.'

She knew that she was playing for time, trying to think it through. It had come as such a shock that Greg was proposing the very thing she wanted most in the world. But she had no right to go ahead until she'd told him the full story. 'He has a right to know'— that relentless phrase that kept on repeating itself in her mind.

'Greg, let's discuss it later, shall we?'

She saw the look of disappointment in his eyes.

'What's there to discuss?'

A waitress was standing behind them waiting to remove the plates.

He pulled a wry face. 'OK, we'll talk as soon as we get back tonight.'

The plates were removed. Chicken and vegetable dishes were being placed around them. Over the clattering and chattering it was impossible to hold a private discussion.

'I'm supposed to be staying another night with my

friend Josie,' Lindy said. 'My car and all my things are over there at her farm.'

'No problem. I'll drive you over there to collect them.'

The desserts arrived—apple pie or profiteroles. Lindy said that she couldn't eat another thing.

The wedding cake was cut. Lindy forced a couple of crumbs down her throat, washed down with a few sips of champagne. She noticed that Greg hadn't drunk anything except mineral water. Good! She wanted him stone-cold sober when she dropped her bombshell.

The speeches seemed endless, but at long last the bride and groom got up to leave.

One of the distant relatives asked Lindy if she knew where the happy couple were spending their honeymoon, and she said she didn't know.

'Cragdale, isn't it?' whispered Greg as the elderly aunt moved away.

Lindy smiled. 'Shh! We're not supposed to know they had their honeymoon at Christmas. Let's keep the marriage idea bright and shiny. No need to disillusion the traditionalists.'

Greg took hold of her arm and began to draw her away. 'Brad told me he was going to spend the next few days decorating the new nursery,' he said quietly.

'That's what marriage is all about,' Lindy said evenly as she began psyching herself up for the revelation that she was going to make just as soon as she could get Greg alone.

But not in the car! she told herself as she watched Greg staring ahead at the bumpy road as he negotiated a hairpin bend. She convinced herself that it wasn't an excuse. She needed his undivided attention.

She began to feel nervous and apprehensive as they turned the corner and the farm came into view. She had to think of a way of keeping Greg away from Josie before they'd had their discussion.

'Better not drive into the farmyard. It's very muddy and it would be a shame to get this car all messed up,' she said quickly.

'I don't mind.'

She could see the gates were open.

'It's better if you turn round at the edge of the field here and go straight back to Moortown. I'll gather my things together and see you as soon as I get back to hospital. I drive much slower than you,' she finished lamely.

He continued to drive towards the gates. 'Anyone would think you were trying to get rid of me. I don't mind how slowly you drive back to Moortown. I think we should go back together.'

'Don't go through into the farmyard, Greg,' she said in desperation. 'They've got free-range hens all over the place and. . .'

Greg slowly inched the car through the gates, making a great play of looking around him until he stopped in front of the kitchen window.

He put his hand across the back of her seat as he pulled her towards him so that their lips could meet in a long, sensual kiss.

'Not a hen in sight,' he murmured, with a wry grin as he pulled away. 'Come on, Lindy; you've got that look again. What are you up to? Why didn't you want me to come here? Is this where you're hiding a dark secret? A husband and children, perhaps?'

He was only joking at first, but Lindy could see that suddenly he was worried.

'Lindy, you're back! I didn't recognise the car. Why don't you both come inside?' Josie called as she bounded out through the kitchen door, drying her hands down the side of her corduroy riding breeches.

'My friend has to get back to hospital,' Lindy began, looking imploringly at Greg. Surely he'd got the message by now?

'No, I don't,' he said, climbing out of the car. 'Hello, I'm Greg.'

Lindy felt her knees wobble as she put her feet to the ground. Out of the corner of her eye she could see Greg, his most captivating smile on his face, his hand outstretched towards Josie.

Josie's welcoming manner had suddenly changed, but Greg took hold of her hand anyway.

'Charming place you have here,' he said, looking around him admiringly. 'Always thought if I hadn't gone into medicine I'd have liked to be a farmer.'

Josie was looking worried and mystified. 'Are you, by any chance, Greg Dalton?'

Greg's eyes barely flickered. 'Fame at last! So Lindy's been talking about me.'

'Not recently,' Josie said coolly, her eyes looking from one to the other of them. 'I didn't think it could be you because you both looked so happy just now in the car. I was looking out of the window, and when I saw you I thought, Oh, good, Lindy's brought her boyfriend and—'

'Josie, there's something I have to tell you,' Lindy began, willing her friend not to say anything else until she'd explained.

'But it's so obvious now,' Josie went on relentlessly. 'You've got back together again and Lindy's told you everything. Were you surprised, Greg, when you heard about—?'

'Don't!' screamed Lindy. 'I haven't told Greg anything yet.'

'Well, I think you should!' Josie said. 'After all, it concerns both of you, doesn't it? Has he any idea what he put you through, Lindy?'

Lindy put her face in her hands. It was like a bad dream. There was no stopping Josie when she felt strongly about something. She'd climbed on her high horse and she wouldn't come down until she'd had her say.

'Do you realise just how much Lindy suffered after her miscarriage, Dr Greg Dalton?' Josie shouted.

'Miscarriage?' Greg looked stunned. 'Was it. . . .?'

Lindy nodded. 'Yes, it was yours. I was three months pregnant when—'

'You were three months and you hadn't told me?' His voice rose to a crescendo. 'Didn't you think I had a right to know I was going to be a father? Didn't it occur to you that I'd want to take care of my own baby? You know how I feel about children. Lindy, how could you keep it to yourself like that?'

Suddenly he paused, drawing in his breath as if trying to overcome the effects of the shock he'd received. His voice was gentle and calm as he continued, 'Lindy, I'm sorry you suffered but you should have told me. I would have—'

'What on earth's going on out here?' Josie's father was standing at the kitchen door looking utterly perplexed. 'Why don't you all come inside?'

'I have to get back to hospital, sir,' Greg said evenly as he opened the car door.

Sam White went back inside the kitchen, shaking his head. He'd no idea what was going on but it didn't concern him. The young people would sort it out between them.

'I'll get my things, Josie,' Lindy began.

'Stay as long as you like,' Greg said. The expression in his eyes as they focused on her was one of hurt and bewilderment. 'You're not on duty till Monday.'

'I'll be back in hospital this evening,' she said firmly.

'I want to explain what happened. I was going to tell you before but—'

She stopped in mid-sentence. All her previous attempts at hiding the truth seemed so futile now. Why hadn't she brought it all out into the open before? He would have been angry, but not as furious as he looked now, behind the wheel of his car.

'I'm sorry, Lindy,' Josie said quietly as Greg's car roared off down the narrow track. 'I'd no idea—'

'It's not your fault, Josie,' Lindy said wearily. 'I should have told him. I suppose it was bound to come out sooner or later. I just wanted to choose my time, that's all.

'You see, his ex-wife kept secrets from him; he desperately wanted to start a family but she stayed on the Pill without telling him. The final straw was when he found out she was having an affair with his best friend. He was so devastated that it was a full six months before he wanted to start living a normal life again. The evening he decided he ought to begin picking up the threads again was the evening we first met. . .the evening I got pregnant.'

'He's much nicer than I imagined,' Josie said subdued. 'I hated him so much for putting you through hell so I just had to let fly at him when I realised who he was. But now I wish I hadn't. He was the man you were telling me about last night, wasn't he? The one you're in love with?'

Lindy nodded, not trusting herself to speak.

'Do you think you'll be able to get back together again?' Josie asked tentatively.

Lindy could feel nothing but emotional agony and uncertainty. 'I don't know,' she said quietly. 'But I'm certainly going to give it a whirl.'

CHAPTER NINE

THERE was no reply when Lindy phoned Greg's room in the residents' quarters. She tried the pink house. The answering machine told her that Dr Dalton couldn't come to the phone right now, but if she left her name and number. . .

She put the phone down. After hurrying back to hospital from the Lakes down a crowded weekend motorway she suddenly felt absolutely whacked.

If Greg wanted to remain unobtainable tonight, she would let him. She wasn't going to chase after him. Let him come to her in his own good time. He'd had a shock and he needed time to recover. Let him get over the first part of the story before she told him the other half. He still didn't know that she'd gone swimming against medical advice on the day she'd lost the baby.

She shivered. Her room seemed unusually cold this evening. She'd turned off the heating before leaving last night but now she needed some warmth and comfort. She fiddled with the thermostat, then, climbing into bed, she snuggled under the duvet, wishing that there was a pair of strong arms wrapped tightly around her.

Her phone was ringing. What time was it? she wondered. The light through the chink in her curtains was pale. She felt completely disorientated as she picked up the phone and answered with a sleepy 'Yes?'

'Lindy?'

She was instantly awake at the sound of Greg's voice.

'Greg. Where—?'

'I know it's your weekend off but could you work a couple of hours this morning? Bill Sutcliffe's just called to say three of the embryos are now in peak condition and he wants us to do the implant as soon as possible. I've phoned Donna and she's on her way here; as you know, we're short-staffed due to Easter and the wedding. Rona would have assisted me but she's not due in till this afternoon.'

'How did you know I'd be here?' Lindy said, climbing out of bed, the phone tucked against her shoulder.

There was a pause. 'I took a chance. I hoped you would be. So can you help or. . .?'

'I'll be in the treatment room in about half an hour. OK?'

'Thanks.'

Oh, he was being so polite, so professional that nothing was going to ruffle his cool, she thought as she showered. But that was what they both needed at the moment—a spell of organised, professional work together, until they'd both calmed down and could talk about their personal life again.

To think he'd actually proposed to her yesterday! It already seemed years ago. Today the rift between them was wider than it had ever been.

Donna was already lying on the treatment-room table when Lindy arrived. Staff Midwife Jean Smith from Nightingale was checking the sterile instruments on the trolley. Bill Sutcliffe was standing alongside, guarding the precious embryos.

Lindy scrubbed up before Jean helped her into a sterile gown.

Greg was already scrubbed and gowned when he arrived. He nodded briefly to his colleagues but his usual easygoing manner wasn't there. He appeared distant, intent only on doing the important treatment without any of the social frills. Only with the patient was he friendly. Certainly he took no more notice of Lindy than he did of the rest of the team.

'As you know, Donna, three embryos are now ready to be put back into your womb. Dr Cash is going to have a look to see if we can go ahead.'

While Lindy was examining the patient's vagina, Greg transferred the embryos into fine plastic tubing in which he'd also placed a minute drop of culture fluid. He handed this to Lindy; carefully she inserted the tube through the cervix, holding it steady while Greg slowly and gently squirted the precious fluid into the womb.

'Are you OK, Donna?' Greg asked.

'Fine, Doctor. When are you going to put the embryos inside me?'

Greg smiled, and Lindy, watching him, thought it was like the sun coming out after a stormy day.

'We've finished. They're inside your womb now, all three of them. Just lie still for a few minutes to let them settle into their new home and then—fingers crossed—we'll hope they decide to stay there. As I told you before, it's unlikely they'll all turn into fully fledged babies. We'll hope for one or even two at the end of all this. When you come back in a couple of weeks we should be able to see if the implantation has been successful.'

'Thanks. You've all been so wonderful to me.'

'I have to warn you that you may be disappointed,' Greg said. 'We may have to go through all this again.'

'I'll just keep on till I'm successful,' Donna said firmly. 'Can Dave come in now to keep me company?'

'Of course,' Lindy said, peeling off her gown and putting it in the bin. 'I'll be passing by the waiting room in a couple of minutes so I'll ask him to come along.'

She was halfway down the corridor when she heard the familiar footsteps behind her. She would have recognised that tread anywhere—firm, decisive, fast. But she didn't turn round until he was right beside her outside the waiting room.

Putting her head round the door, she told Donna's husband that he could go along to the treatment room.

'Am I a father yet?' he asked, smiling.

'Hopefully, you're on your way,' Lindy said.

Greg was waiting for her, an enigmatic expression on his face.

'I've been thinking,' he said slowly as they walked together through into the hospital. 'Maybe I was a bit hasty last night. I suppose in a way I was shell-shocked. As I drove back I began to think that the miscarriage must have been pretty awful for you. Josie said you'd suffered.'

'Oh, yes, I suffered,' she said, holding back the emotion. 'Look, we can't talk about it here.'

'Let's go and walk on the hills, somewhere where we won't be disturbed. We can shout at each other as much as we like and only the sheep will hear us,' he said, with a wry grin.

She smiled, relieved to find that Greg's sense of humour was coming back. 'I think that would be a good idea. Clear the air.'

'Ten minutes?' he asked.

She nodded. 'I'll find my walking boots and see you in the car park.'

There were a few rain-clouds threatening to spoil the blue Easter Sunday sky as they walked the stony path high above Cragdale. Greg had suggested that they leave the car at his house and follow the track behind it.

They hadn't even gone into the house for a coffee.

He'd seemed in a hurry to climb up onto the fells and get on with their discussion.

But at the back of Lindy's mind, as she tramped along behind him on the narrow trail, was the thought that if they managed to sort out their problems up here among the hills they would be free to go back to the house, hopefully in a better frame of mind. And if they went into the house they would get back together again.

Looking at Greg's broad back, she wondered if he was thinking the same thing. They could have walked anywhere in the Dales but he'd chosen to have the pink house as a base, and that was a good sign that he was hoping for a reconciliation.

At the point where the path dipped down into the next valley Greg stopped and brushed his hand over the surface of a craggy boulder.

'How about this for the discussion chamber?'

'Looks OK to me,' she said, sitting down. The morning sun had warmed the stone. It wasn't comfortable but the view was good. A near panorama of hills stretching as far as the eye could see made her feel more relaxed; yes, at last she was in the mood to straighten things out between Greg and herself once and for all. After all, she'd got nothing to lose now that the cat was out of the bag.

He was only inches away from her, his fingers pressed firmly against the surface of the rock. She turned to look at him and was temporarily put off by the stern expression on his face. He didn't look in any way approachable.

She cleared her throat. 'I would have told you sooner but—'

'Just tell me now,' he said with ominous calm. 'Explain how you came to decide a couple of years ago that you wouldn't tell me you were carrying my baby.'

Suddenly all the pent-up frustration she was feeling burst out. 'I would have thought that was obvious! The day after we'd been together a friend told me you were married. I was furious you'd deceived me. When I knew I was pregnant I didn't even think you'd be interested; a married man who—'

'Not be interested!' he flung back at her, his knuckles whitening as he gripped the rock. 'You could have made a phone call to find out. Even when we met up again here in Moortown and you found out the truth about my marriage you still continued to keep me in the dark.'

'Well, then we're both quits, aren't we?' she said quietly. 'We've both deceived each other.'

For a few minutes they sat side by side without speaking, without touching—inches away from each other but miles apart. Only the sound of the curlews wheeling overhead and the occasional bleating of a sheep disturbed what should have been an idyllic setting.

Greg was the first to speak. 'Look, we're both being too stubborn about this.'

Lindy felt his arm pulling her against him. For an instant she stiffened, still too proud to give in, but his familiar charisma softened her. She turned to look at him and he put a hand under her chin.

'Let's start again, shall we?' Very slowly he brought his lips down onto hers.

She remained very still, savouring the moment of reconciliation, hoping that it wasn't going to be a temporary truce when the full revelations were made. She had to tell him; if they were going to get together on a permanent basis, there must be no secrets standing between them. But how could she find the right words? Where should she start so that she could soften the blow? A little voice in her head told her to go for it, head on. She'd put it off for far too long. The longer she left it, the harder it would become.

'The miscarriage was a traumatic experience,' she began quietly. 'I recovered physically, but mentally I was haunted with guilt. I—'

'Guilt? Lindy, you didn't. . .?'

'No, no, of course I didn't do anything to bring on the miscarriage. . .I mean, not intentionally.' She took a deep breath. 'I loved that baby more than anything in the world. I could never have harmed it.'

She saw the flickering of his eyes as his expression changed. 'So why the guilt?' he asked evenly.

She hesitated. 'I thought my obstetrician was being over-cautious when he advised me not to swim until I was three months pregnant. As far as I knew there was no clinical reason to insist on this. I felt so fit and well. I thought nothing could go wrong. So. . .just before the third month, I went swimming with my half-sister Lucy and. . .and I started to bleed. . .so she called the ambulance and. . .'

Greg cradled her against his chest as the tears began to fall. 'My poor darling. It must have been awful for you.'

She pulled her head away from his sweater and looked up into his dark, troubled eyes.

'You're not angry? Not mad at me for being stupid?'

Greg's gentle reaction wasn't what she'd expected and she didn't know how to take it. Somehow she felt it was the calm before the storm. The expression in his eyes was one of shock and bewilderment. He was saying comforting words but she could tell that deep down his emotions were in turmoil. This latest shock had floored him.

He hesitated. 'I'm disappointed, but I don't want to make you suffer any more,' he said in an expressionless voice. 'Let's say I'm sad you lost the baby but I wish you'd taken more care of yourself.'

'I knew that's what you'd think! I was scared of telling you before because I knew your disappointment would only add to my feeling of guilt.'

'Lindy, stop torturing yourself! You've been through a trying time, but let's be rational about this. Did you have a full investigation of the miscarriage? Did your obstetrician collect up the foetal material for analysis?'

She shuddered as the memories came flooding back. The stabbing pains as she'd swum across the pool, dragging herself into the pool-house, wrapping herself in towels as she'd writhed in pain on the floor. Lucy phoning for the ambulance, her mother bending over her, throwing away the soaked towels and wrapping her in fresh ones. . .

'It wasn't possible. Anyway, I just wanted to forget it at the time. When the obstetrician gave me a final examination and said I was OK to leave hospital I never went back. I thought he would have contacted me if he'd thought there was anything I should know.'

'Not necessarily,' Greg said with steely calm.

'Well, that's what we'd do here at Moortown,' she said defensively.

'Are you sure you didn't lose touch with your obstetrician on purpose because you knew he wouldn't approve of the way you'd ignored his advice?'

She drew in her breath. She'd never thought about it before, but Greg had hit the nail right on the head.

'Maybe,' she whispered, half to herself.

'Lindy, if only you'd told me!'

'Stop it, Greg; we're going round in circles! We can't turn the clock back! This is why I didn't tell you before, because I knew you'd be angry.'

'And do you blame me? If only I could have been

with you, to take care of you. The baby might—'

'Don't, Greg!' His words were like a knife being twisted inside her.

'I'm sorry.' He held her against him until she stopped trembling. 'Let's go home,' he whispered.

As she walked behind him down the rough path behind the pink house she could sense his sadness by the droop of his shoulders. His anger might have turned to disappointment, he might have forgiven her, but could she ever forgive herself?

Would it help if she faced up to her obstetrician and got the full facts as Greg had suggested? Maybe she'd been burying her head in the sand for too long and now was the time to face up to the truth, whatever that might be.

She remembered how she hadn't been able to make out the foetus from where she'd been lying on the couch, some way from the screen, at that final ultrasound examination. She remembered how Alex Grainger had walked in front of the screen and switched it off.

At the time she'd thought that he was simply very busy. She knew the feeling when patients held her up with endless questions. And she had been due to have another scan the following week so she'd planned to ask for more time in front of the screen and less in consultation.

Yes, she ought to find out why he'd been so over-cautious with her. She'd assumed that this was his normal way of working but perhaps there had been some other reason.

As they sat at the kitchen table drinking tea and eating toasted cheese sandwiches, Lindy told Greg what she'd decided.

'I'll phone Lucy in the States and see if my obstetrician still works in the same hospital. I'd like to contact him.'

Greg nodded. 'You could do that; although it's a bit late now—more than two years since you were a patient and you didn't have any follow-up appointments.'

She looked away. He sounded uncharacteristically despondent. She'd hoped for some kind of relief once she'd shared her secret and her guilt with Greg, but it had only made it worse.

He put his hand over hers. 'Come to bed and let's forget our differences. That's the only place we're ever in total agreement.'

The last thing she felt like was passionate love-making!

'Greg, I think I'd like to go back to hospital. It's all been so exhausting and—'

He reached across to put a finger over her lips. 'Shh. We've been fighting long enough. Let's have a truce.'

Her body responded as she saw the tenderness in his eyes. He was standing up, coming round the table to pull her to her feet. And then he was lifting her up, his arms strong and muscular underneath her.

She knew that the exhaustion she'd felt was merely emotional. He carried her upstairs, pushed open the bedroom door with his knee, and laying her gently down on the four-poster bed, deftly undid her zips and buttons.

Her sensual excitement began to mount as his fingers caressed her bare skin, gently at first, and then more passionately. The hardness of his arousal, pressing against the soft curves of her body, sent shivers of raw passion deep inside her.

As his tantalising tongue and fingers caressed her she moved her hands over his hard, resilient, virile body, straining against him, until the moment came when he entered her and she gave an ecstatic cry of fulfilment. Slowly at first and then more vigorously he moved inside her, driving her sensual excitement higher and higher until the final, delirious climax.

Afterwards she lay back in the crook of his arm, feeling relaxed and invigorated at the same time. She knew that she would always love Greg whatever happened, but, looking up into his eyes, she could see that strange, enigmatic expression again. He was still suffering from the shock of what she'd told him.

But had he forgiven her? And how would he feel if the miscarriage had scarred her permanently? She'd had patients who'd become sterile after a miscarriage. This awful thought had been at the back of her mind for so long. She'd shelved it, thinking the answer unimportant as she forged ahead with her career. But now, when there was a real chance of them getting together, could she put Greg through the uncertainty of not knowing whether she would be able to give him a child?

He'd told her that he adored children. He wanted a family. She had to find out if she would be able to have another baby. She had to get in touch with her obstetrician as soon as possible. And there was no time like the present!

She climbed out of the four-poster and went over to the bathroom.

'I need to get back to hospital,' she said quietly, wrapping herself in Greg's huge towelling robe.

He seemed surprised. 'Do you have to? I mean—'

'I've got loads of things to do before tomorrow.'

He was climbing off the bed, looking handsomely rugged, and ruffled from their lovemaking. 'Such as?' he drawled in a husky voice as he reached out for her.

She evaded his grasp. 'Oh, I don't want to bore you with my long list of chores.'

He gave her a wry grin. 'OK, Doctor; I can see

you're in a working mood so I won't try to detain you. I'll drive you back as soon as you're ready. But Lindy. . .'

'Yes?'

'You didn't give me your answer yesterday.'

She tied the knot of the robe tighter, her fingers beginning to tremble. 'I need time to think.'

'About what? Surely—'

'Greg, I need to find out why my obstetrician was being so careful with me. If there's something gynaecologically wrong with me, I need to know before. . . before I can think about marriage.'

He came across the room in easy strides and took her in his arms as she held back the tears.

'I want to be able to give you children. I know how important it is for you to have a family, Greg, and—'

'Darling, you're everything I want. A family would be wonderful but—'

'You say that now, in the first flush of romance, but how would you feel after a few years without children?'

'Lindy, we'll cross each bridge as we come to it,' he said patiently. 'First, let's find out if you were harmed by the miscarriage and—'

'And if I'm sterile. . .?' she said in a small voice as she looked up into his troubled eyes.

'Well, then. . .we'll take the next step. Check out all the possibilities. After all, we're working in the right department,' he finished.

'That's true.' She gave an involuntary shiver as she thought of all the couples who were unsuccessful in their infertility treatment. The years of treatment, the disappointment when they were finally told that there was no hope of their having a baby.

If that happened to Greg and her would they consider adoption? There were very few babies for adoption now and, anyway, she wanted her own child. . . Greg's child. If she couldn't give him a child then she didn't want to go ahead with the marriage. She couldn't stand years of knowing that she'd deprived him of the family he longed for.

She eased herself out of Greg's arms. 'Got to go,' she whispered, reaching up to kiss the side of his cheek.

He tilted her face and kissed her gently on the lips. 'Don't worry until you've found out all the facts.'

She nodded. But as she stepped into the shower she knew that she couldn't help worrying.

They were both quiet, deep in their own thoughts, on the journey back to Moortown. Greg dropped her off at the car park and turned straight round to go back to Cragdale.

Back in her room Lindy went straight to the phone and dialled her mother's number in the States. The answering machine replied.

She put the phone down without leaving a message. She would wait until she knew that she could speak to Lucy. Try again tomorrow. It was something of an anticlimax but at least she'd taken the first step. She would cross each bridge as she came to it, as Greg had told her; and she would try not to look too far ahead, just in case it was bad news.

Easter Monday was quiet in hospital, but Lindy had to see patients on Nightingale. Greg didn't have to come in. He'd told her that he would spend the day out at Cragdale. As she walked down the ward, checking on the new mothers and babies, at the back of her mind she had a picture of Greg sitting in his kitchen, the sun streaming in through the windows.

Deliberately she made an effort to banish the image. She had to concentrate on the patients.

Sister Gregson was back on duty after her weekend

in the Lake District at Sara's wedding. She invited Lindy into her office for coffee at the end of the ward round.

'Didn't Sara look lovely?' Ann Gregson said as she handed a cup to Lindy. 'You know, I'd like to feel that, in some way, I've been instrumental in getting Sara and Bradley Prestcot together. I used to invite them both in here for a coffee, and then I'd watch them going off together down the corridor. Their hands would touch and I'd see them smiling at each other. Oh, it was so romantic! I could hear wedding bells right from the start, even though they seemed to have their problems like all couples do before they decide to get married.'

Lindy took a sip of her coffee as she watched Sister Gregson's animated expression. 'You're quite a romantic, aren't you, Sister?'

'Oh, yes. I've always got my head in a romantic novel when I'm off duty. Still, I suppose reading is no substitute for the real thing, is it?

'I was going to get married once; I was twenty-one. I'd just qualified and he was a clerk in the hospital administration department; later on he became Mayor of Moortown, would you believe, and got a knighthood for his services to the community. But when I went out with him he was just a clerk.

'Anyway, we quarrelled about something. I honestly can't remember what it was now. But he was so stubborn; he wouldn't say he was sorry and I was damned—pardon the expression, dear—if I would give in when it was all his fault. We were two of a kind, I suppose—both too proud to climb down. Anyway, we were busy with our careers and we just drifted apart.'

Lindy felt a lump rising in her throat as she watched the faraway expression on Ann's face. Greg had been right about this outwardly daunting sister. She'd certainly had her moments.

Sister Gregson blinked and gave an embarrassed smile. 'Can't think why I'm telling you all this.'

Neither could Lindy; it didn't help to hear what had happened to a couple who'd drifted apart.

'I've never told anyone about it before,' Ann said. 'They all think I'm an old fuddy-duddy, but inside I'm just as young as I always was.'

She swept a hand over the greying curl that had escaped from the side of her starched, frilly white cap.

'Anyway, I don't regret it. I've had a good career as well as a romance. I think it's quite true, that old saying that it's better to have loved and lost than never to have loved at all.'

Neither of them spoke for a few seconds. Lindy could hear the outside buzz of the ward, a baby crying, a couple of mothers chatting. Here in the relative calm of Ann Gregson's office she had time to take stock.

In years to come would she be able to be so philosophical about her relationship with Greg if they didn't marry? Would she be able to say calmly what Sister had just said? 'Loved and lost'.

'I'm probably chatting like this because weddings seem to be in the air on Nightingale,' Sister said, warming once more to her subject. 'First there was Hannah and Simon, then Sara and Bradley, and I do believe. . .a little bird told me—'

She broke off, a half-smile on her lips, her head on one side, as if appealing to Lindy to finish the sentence with some kind of announcement.

Lindy swallowed hard. 'What did a little bird tell you, Sister?'

'That's all right, my dear. If you don't want to talk about it then—'

'You're right. I don't want to talk about it,' Lindy

said, standing up. 'But thanks for the coffee, Sister, and the chat.'

'I could tell there was something on your mind, dear,' Sister Gregson said, moving over to her desk. 'What I was really getting at was that I'd hate to see you and Greg break up like Jack and I did.'

Sir Jack Hamilton, chairman of the board! Knighted for services to the community. Of course! The man who'd grilled her so meticulously at her interview.

Ann Gregson's eyes were twinkling as she watched Lindy's incredulous expression.

'And you'd better keep that under your hat.'

Lindy gave her a conspiratorial smile. 'Don't worry, Sister. Your secret's safe with me.'

As soon as she got off duty in the evening she kicked off her shoes, stretched out on the bed and picked up her phone. Within seconds she could hear that it was ringing at the other end, and in her mind's eye she could see quite clearly the little white-painted wooden bungalow beside the sea on Cape Cod. She glanced at her watch, five hours' difference in time; it would still be early afternoon over there.

She smiled as she recognised her mother's voice, slightly breathless as if she'd hurried to the phone.

'Lindy! What a lovely surprise! We're sitting out in the garden having lunch and we were just talking about you.'

'I must be psychic,' Lindy said. 'Mum, is Lucy there?'

'She certainly is. She came out from hospital for the Easter weekend. I'll get her for you.'

'Lucy, are you still in contact with Alex Grainger?' Lindy asked after they'd both chatted inconsequentially for a couple of minutes.

'The obstetrician?'

Lindy heard the surprise in her half-sister's voice.

'Yes, I need to speak to him.'

'Lindy, you're not. . .?'

'No, of course not! It's something connected with my work.'

The white lie slipped out very easily. She justified it by telling herself that she didn't want Lucy to get involved at this stage. Lucy's opinion of Greg was the same as Josie's, and Lindy had deliberately not mentioned the fact that they'd met up again.

'He left the hospital about a year ago. Is it important? Couldn't somebody else help you? I mean, come on, Lindy, I'm not stupid. I assume this has something to do with your miscarriage.'

Lindy hesitated. Lucy could read her like a book! She should have known that she couldn't pull the wool over her eyes. But how much should she tell her? Certainly, she shouldn't mention Greg.

'OK, I'll come clean, Lucy. Yes, it concerns the miscarriage. I want some medical information about it.'

'At last!' Lucy sounded excited.

'How do you mean, "at last"?'

'Alex Grainger told me this might happen. He said that a lot of his patients can't bear to discuss the subject of their miscarriage. They close their minds to it, try to pretend it didn't happen. You were like that. He was worried when you went back to England so soon afterwards. He said that if ever you brought up the subject again I was to let him know. But you never did, and I don't imagine he'll be able to help you now that it's more than two years since—'

'But do you know where Alex Grainger went?'

'No idea, but I'll try to find out for you.'

'Bless you; but Lucy, don't tell Mum. She'll only worry. You remember what she was like when I had the miscarriage. That's why I had to get back to

England so quickly and go and stay with Josie. I couldn't stand the constant fuss and worry, not to mention the endless questions.'

'There's nothing to tell,' Lucy replied breezily. 'Bye.'

As Lindy put the phone down she knew instinctively that Lucy was annoyed because she obviously hadn't been told the whole story. She hated upsetting her dear, kind sister, but it would have upset her even more if she'd known that Lindy was having an affair with the man who'd caused so much suffering.

Lindy was back in the infertility unit again next morning, working side by side with Greg in the treatment room. There were several routine infertility tests, a couple of IVF implantations to perform and one donor insemination.

The donor insemination came last on the list, just before the lunch break. Lindy settled the patient's husband in the waiting room, after making sure that he was in agreement with what was going to happen to his wife.

Greg was drawing up the donor semen into fine plastic tubing when she returned to the treatment room.

'Is Keith OK?' asked the patient on the table. 'He was more nervous than I was this morning when we were getting ready to come in. I said, Look, don't worry. There's nothing you can do about it, and he took offence at that.'

Lindy joined Greg on the other side of the table and looked down at their patient.

'I think he's feeling a bit helpless about the whole situation, Cathy,' Lindy said quietly.

She remembered the first time that Cathy and Keith Cross had come to the clinic. They'd gone through all the routine tests to see why Cathy hadn't got pregnant, and it had been discovered that there were absolutely no sperm in Keith's semen. He'd taken it pretty hard, said he didn't mind being childless, but Cathy had talked him around.

For a while they'd considered adoption but when they'd begun to enquire they'd been told that there were few babies for adoption and a very long waiting list. Eventually Keith had agreed that Cathy should have donor insemination.

'Keith's afraid the baby will love me more than him,' Cathy said.

'I told Keith that to all intents and purposes he'll be the baby's father,' Greg said gently. 'From the time your baby is born he'll be there, taking care of it with you. We've been very careful in selecting a donor with the same colour hair and eyes.'

'Can you tell me anything more about him, Doctor,' Cathy asked.

Greg shook his head. 'We don't give out that kind of information. Most probably the sperm was donated by a healthy young medical student. Now, if you'd just like to relax, Cathy. . .'

Carefully Greg inserted the fine tubing through the patient's cervix before very gently squirting the precious fluid into the womb.

'Keep still for a few minutes, Cathy, and then you'll be free to go.' Greg said. 'If Keith's still worried about something—anything at all—come back and see me. In any case I'd like to examine you in a month's time to see if we've been successful.'

'Would you have a word with Keith, now, Dr Dalton?' Cathy said in a pleading tone. 'Just tell him it's nobody's fault he couldn't make me pregnant. I think it was probably that awful bout of German measles he had when he was twenty-three.'

'I'll go and see him now,' Greg said.

Lindy was already pulling off her gown; she planned to spend a quiet half-hour in her room, with her feet up and an apple. The idea of lunch in the noisy canteen seemed unappealing, to say the least. And if Greg was going to listen to Keith pouring his heart out he wouldn't be able to get away for ages.

Back in her room she kicked off her shoes and lay on the bed.

The wretched phone was ringing.

'Look, I'm trying to take half an hour off. . .' she began, but didn't finish her sentence when she heard the switchboard operator break in to say,

'I'm so sorry to disturb you in your room, Dr Cash, but I've got your sister on the line. She's phoned twice this morning and I said you couldn't be disturbed in the work you were doing. You're through now, caller. . .'

'Lindy, I've been trying to get you—

'Have you got some news about Alex Grainger?'

'He took a post in a hospital in London and now he's got his own private clinic.'

'London, Ontario?' Lindy queried.

'No, London, England.'

'But that's great! Do you know the name of his clinic?'

'No, but I was told it's in some sort of street where all the posh consultants have consulting rooms.'

'Harley Street?'

'Could be. I wouldn't know. You'll have to check it out, Lindy.'

Someone was knocking on the door.

'Thanks. You're the best little sister I could possibly wish for. Sorry, Lucy, I'll have to go; there's someone at the door. Come in!'

'But you don't trust me enough to tell me what this is all about,' Lucy persisted.

Lindy still cradled the phone as the door opened and Greg walked in. He eased himself down into an armchair and mouthed for her to carry on with her conversation.

'Don't mind me,' he whispered, picking up a medical journal.

'Lucy, I've got to go; someone's arrived.'

'And has that someone got anything to do with this sudden interest in your obstetrician?'

'Sorry, Lucy, I don't want to answer that. Thanks again for your help. Bye.'

Greg looked up. 'Was that your sister?'

'Yes, she's tracked down Alex Grainger, my obstetrician. He's got a private clinic in London, probably in or near Harley Street.'

He stood up and crossed the room, leaning over her on the bed as she lay back against the pillows. He kissed her tenderly on the lips. She put up her hands and ran her fingers through his hair.

'Suddenly it seems very important to put the past behind me, and I can't do that until I know the full truth,' she said quietly.

He sat down on the bed and took hold of her hands, kissing the tips of her fingers. She remained very still, savouring the sensual moment.

'You've got to realise that he'll probably have forgotten all about you,' Greg said gently. 'It's more than two years since and he won't have any of your records.'

'I'll have to take that chance,' Lindy said. 'My hunch is that he'll remember me. Lucy told me he'd instructed her to contact him if ever I wanted to know more about my miscarriage. He didn't want to impose the details on me unless I asked for them. He said it was quite common for patients not to want to know.'

'But you're a doctor, Lindy,' Greg said, dropping her hands as he stood up and walked over to the window. 'Didn't you want to know all the medical details?'

His back was towards her; she couldn't see his expression but she heard the exasperation in his tone.

'I didn't feel like a doctor,' she whispered. 'I felt like a helpless child. Nothing mattered any more. I wanted to die.'

'Darling, I'm sorry!' Greg rushed back to take her in his arms. 'If only I could have been with you everything would have been different. I'd have insisted we find out the full facts there and then.'

He was stroking her hair, nuzzling his face against hers, his lips gently kissing her cheek.

Suddenly he pulled away, a concerned expression in his eyes. 'You say this Alex Grainger told Lucy to contact him if you wanted more information?'

A cold hand seemed to be clutching at her heart when she looked at Greg's troubled face.

'You're thinking what I'm thinking, aren't you, Greg?'

He hesitated. 'I suppose, as doctors, we've reached the same rational conclusion. There was obviously something about your case that he would have told you if you'd wanted to know.'

She swallowed hard. 'It certainly seems that way.'

'Well, the sooner we track down this Alex Grainger the better,' Greg said firmly.

CHAPTER TEN

ALEX GRAINGER'S clinic was in a tall, terraced house set back from the road. At the other side of the road in the small London square the May blossom was out, and sparrows hopped from branch to branch, chattering excitedly.

Their taxi pulled away from the kerb, leaving Lindy standing with Greg on the pavement; she was relieved that they'd actually arrived. It hadn't been as easy as she'd hoped to track down Alex Grainger.

The obstetrician was one of four partners in the clinic and its name gave no indication that he worked here. Coupled with the fact that the clinic was several streets away from Harley Street, it had required some dedicated detective work on the part of Greg. If he hadn't made numerous phone calls to friends and colleagues in London they might not have been standing here now.

They'd come down from Moortown by train that morning, leaving very early while the hospital was still in the capable hands of the night staff. But even at that early hour their departure together hadn't gone unnoticed. They'd had to run the gauntlet of pointed remarks from medical friends and colleagues as they'd climbed into the taxi that had taken them to the Moortown station.

It had taken two weeks to track down Alex Grainger and make an appointment. Greg had insisted on coming with Lindy, and had organised the work schedule so that they could both have a couple of days off. They'd stopped off at the hotel that Greg had booked, to leave their luggage on their way to the clinic.

Lindy took a deep breath. 'Let's get this over with.'

Greg put his hand under her arm as they climbed the stone steps together. 'Nervous?' he asked gently.

She nodded. 'Petrified.'

Greg squeezed her arm. 'Now you know how our patients feel. We may think it's only a simple examination but to them it's a huge hurdle.'

'I'll be glad when I've got over this hurdle and seen what's on the other side,' she said quietly as she watched Greg selecting the correct doorbell to press for Alex Grainger.

Seconds later a nurse in white dress and cap arrived at the door to let them in.

'Mr Grainger is ready for you, Dr Cash,' she told Lindy, before turning to smile at Greg and say, 'Would you like to sit in the waiting room, sir?'

'No, I'd prefer to come along with Dr Cash,' Greg replied without hesitation.

The nurse's eyes flickered. 'May I have your name, sir?'

'Dr Greg Dalton.'

'Thank you, Doctor. If you'd both like to come this way. . .'

Lindy's knees felt decidedly weak as she walked up the impressive stone staircase to the first floor. A thick white carpet stretched along the corridor in front of them. She wondered fleetingly if anyone had ever walked over it with muddy feet. Probably not, in the middle of London. And Alex Grainger probably never dealt with emergencies here—the sort where the patients would be bleeding profusely as they were carried from the ambulance.

She put a hand over her face, trying to blot out the vivid memories of that fateful day when she'd found out what it was really like to be a patient.

'Are you OK, Lindy?' Greg put his arm round her shoulders.

'Yes, I'm fine. Just nervous, that's all.'

'No need to be nervous.' The nurse smiled. 'Alex Grainger is very considerate with his patients and, after all, you're a doctor yourself.'

Lindy counted to ten. It was true that she was a doctor, but she was also a woman who'd been through a traumatic experience when it had been difficult to think straight. Being a doctor didn't mean that she could keep her feelings and emotions on ice.

The nurse took them into a spacious, well-appointed room that overlooked the square, and introduced them to the obstetrician.

Alex Grainger was sitting behind a wide, leather-topped mahogany desk. He stood up to greet them.

'Do sit down.'

He waved a hand towards a couple of leather armchairs in front of his desk. Glancing down at the open file on his desk, he said, 'I've got nothing in the file except your name, Dr Cash. Forgive me, Dr Dalton, but I'm not quite sure why you're here.'

Greg and Lindy both began to speak at the same time, but Lindy insisted that she carry on. 'Please, Greg, let me explain to Mr Grainger. He's obviously forgotten me, and I think I should fill in the details.'

'Forgotten you?' Alex Grainger queried. 'If you're one of my patients the information would be in your file here but—'

'I was a patient of yours at Markham Memorial Hospital,' she said quietly. 'My sister, Lucy Spencer, is a nurse there. Two years ago in June I had a miscarriage and I was rushed in as an emergency.'

She saw the light of recognition dawn in the obstetrician's eyes. 'Lindy Cash, of course. But you look so different now. You're much thinner than you were.'

'And older and wiser,' Lindy quipped, with a nervous smile.

'How is your sister?'

'She's fine.'

'I kept in contact with her but she told me you'd left the family home on Cape Cod and gone back to England, I believe. I didn't want to follow up your case unless I was asked to.'

'That's why I came here,' she said. 'I need to know if there's something I wasn't aware of about my pregnancy and miscarriage.'

Alex Grainger leaned back in his chair, his eyes focusing first on Lindy and then on Greg.

'Is your interest professional or personal, Dr Dalton?'

'Both,' Greg replied evenly. 'Dr Cash is a colleague and I was the father of her unborn child.'

The obstetrician's expression remained impassive as he looked at Lindy. 'I assume there has been a reconciliation. I remember that you told me the father didn't wish to acknowledge his child.'

Lindy saw the pain in Greg's eyes as he turned to look at her.

'I didn't know Lindy was pregnant,' Greg said evenly. 'I was waiting for a divorce from my first wife at the time.'

'Your first wife? So, if you were waiting for a divorce then I presume you're married to each other now.'

'No!' Lindy said.

At the same time Greg said, 'Not yet.'

She gave him a wry smile. If only it was that easy!

'Well, in that case,' Alex Grainger said, 'I'll speak freely in front of both of you. I remember your case very well. You were in good health when you first came to me and I confirmed that you were six weeks pregnant. I gave you a scan and, if you remember, we couldn't see the heartbeat flashing. But we both agreed that six weeks was early to detect this.'

'Mr Grainger, did you detect some abnormality that you didn't tell me about?' Lindy asked.

The obstetrician hesitated. 'Yes, I did. But at six weeks I couldn't be sure. When you came to me at eleven weeks for your next scan my diagnosis was confirmed. You had the chromosomal defect known as trisomy.'

Lindy drew in her breath. 'But that's usually associated with pregnancy in older women. I was only twenty-four.'

'Exactly! That's why I was unwilling to trust my own diagnosis. You were carrying an empty sac instead of a normal embryo. I decided, rightly or wrongly, at six weeks to leave you in the dark until I was absolutely sure. That's why I didn't do any more scans until the diagnosis could be made with certainty.

'At eleven weeks, when you came for what I'd hoped you would think was a routine investigation, there was absolutely no doubt that the trisomy defect was a reality. I knew I would have to do a termination. I asked you to come back a week later, I remember. In the event you were rushed in that same evening. Mother Nature had stepped in to prevent the pregnancy continuing.'

'Mr Grainger,' Greg said icily, 'didn't it occur to you that Lindy might want to know her pregnancy wasn't viable, that there was nothing inside the embryonic sac?'

The obstetrician shifted uncomfortably on his seat. 'It was a calculated risk. I knew Dr Cash would be devastated when I told her. I also hoped that her lover might have turned up to hold her hand when the inevitable happened.'

'"When the inevitable happened",' Lindy repeated,

half to herself. She could feel the burden of guilt slipping away. 'If only I'd known I was carrying an embryo with a trisomy defect I would have realised it wasn't the swimming that caused the miscarriage. I would have lost it anyway. But why did you try to wrap me in cotton wool right from the start? I thought you were the most cautious obstetrician I'd ever met.'

'I couldn't be sure of my diagnosis at six weeks but I had a hunch something was wrong, and I didn't want you to miscarry all on your own while we were waiting to be sure.

'Besides, Lucy had told me she was sure your lover would turn up soon. She assured me that you were still very much in love with the man even though you didn't realise it. I was hoping that was the case. I mean, haven't you found that the partner of a pregnant patient often turns up when they hear about the pregnancy, Dr Cash? I didn't know any details about your affair, but you seemed so happy that I was sure the father would arrive on the scene at some point and would be around to comfort you when the inevitable happened.'

'Better late than never,' Greg said quietly, his voice husky with emotion.

'But too late for that pregnancy, Dr Dalton,' the obstetrician said.

'But not for the next,' Greg said evenly. 'Look, do you think we could dispense with the formalities? I'm Greg; Lindy you know very well and—'

'And I'm Alex; so let's start thinking about the next pregnancy, shall we? Some time in the future I assume you'll want to get pregnant again, Lindy.'

Lindy nodded, not daring to look at Greg.

'So I assume that with your knowledge of obstetrics you're aware of the possibility that there could be a repeat performance of your last pregnancy?'

She nodded again. She'd been so relieved to know that the swimming hadn't been the cause of the miscarriage that she hadn't yet thought the implications through.

'I know that in a woman who's had one miscarriage because of trisomy a second miscarriage is a bit more likely,' she said quietly. 'And a third, even a fourth, but by this time they usually give up. . .and accept the inevitable.'

Greg reached out and put his hand over hers. She could feel the tightening of his fingers as he spoke in a calm, even voice.

'So, we'll have to make sure Lindy is closely monitored during the next pregnancy because there's a slightly increased risk of an abnormal foetus going to full term.'

Alex Grainger nodded in agreement. 'Yes, an amniocentesis would be necessary halfway through the pregnancy. Taking a sample of the fluid surrounding the foetus would give a clear indication if there was any abnormality. Would you like me to give you a full examination now?'

'I think that would be advisable,' Lindy said evenly.

The nurse arrived back to take her through to the examination cubicle. As she lay on the couch, covered by a thin sheet, it seemed strange that she was the patient, on the receiving end of the treatment.

In spite of the warm May morning Alex Grainger's hands were cold as he placed them on her abdomen. Lindy made a mental note to ensure that her own were always warm! She closed her eyes as she tried to relax.

Greg had chosen to go down to the waiting room while she was being examined. He was waiting for her at the foot of the stairs. The nurse opened the door and said goodbye on the steps. Greg took hold of Lindy's arm as they crossed the road.

'Well?' He stood still on the pavement, turning her to face him. 'What was the verdict?'

She took a deep breath. 'As far as Alex can determine, the uterus hasn't been damaged. . .'

'Well, that's a relief.'

'But there's no way of determining whether a chromasomal defect would occur in my foetus if I were to get pregnant so—'

'But we'll have you closely monitored while you're pregnant,' Greg put in quickly. 'We'd pick up on any abnormality and—'

'Greg, I don't want to think too far ahead,' Lindy said quietly. 'One step at a time.'

'Of course. I don't want to put any pressure on you but—'

'Alex says that physically I'm in excellent shape,' she said, tucking her arm through Greg's as she tried desperately to stop him talking about pregnancy. Alex had told her that she must be prepared for a recurrence, that it might be several pregnancies before she successfully produced a child and that she must face the fact that she might never be successful.

'I could have told him that for free!' Greg said. 'I bet he charges exorbitant fees.'

'As a matter of fact there was no charge,' Lindy replied. 'He said he thought he owed me a favour after all I'd been through.'

'Very noble of him. He's a nice enough chap, but I don't want him to take care of you for your next pregnancy. I don't approve of doctors who don't advise their patients about what's going on. There are occasions when you have to wrap it up a bit but, by and large, it's advisable in the long run to come clean. We'll choose somebody nearer home; Brad or Simon would be good. I wouldn't dare take you on. Besides, doctors shouldn't take on their wives as patients because—'

'Greg, stop jumping the gun!'

She stood absolutely still in the middle of the square and turned to face him. 'I can't take all this looking into the future. If I can't be sure I can have children, I can't marry you. It wouldn't be fair. I don't want to take a chance on something that's so important to you.'

He tilted her face up towards him. The midday sun cleft a blazing valley between them, giving her the impression that Greg's head was surrounded with flames. He looked like a mythological god. She closed her eyes to ease the dazzling effect and felt his warm lips pressing against hers.

'I've come to the conclusion that we can never be sure of anything in this life,' he whispered against her hair. 'But I'm willing to take a chance if you are.'

'I don't think marriage should depend on chance,' she said quietly.

A policeman passing through the park was smiling as he glanced at the couple wrapped in each other's arms. A grey squirrel, looking perfectly at home in the middle of the city, ran up an old oak tree and stared down at them from an overhanging branch.

'Lots of people do take a chance,' Greg said.

'And lots of people get divorced,' Lindy said. 'For a variety of reasons. A childless marriage for a couple who love children can be devastating.'

His carefree expression changed. 'We'd always have each other,' he said gently. 'That would be enough for me.'

'That's what you say now,' she whispered. 'If only I could believe you. If only I could be sure.'

Strong emotions churned inside her. She wanted so

desperately to marry him. 'Let's take a walk. I need to think.'

'Don't think too long,' he said firmly. 'I need an answer today.'

He held her close against him as they walked out of the square; they wandered through the London streets hand in hand, totally wrapped up in each other.

There was a burger van parked outside the gates of Regent's Park. Greg bought beefburgers with lashings of onions and doused them liberally in tomato ketchup.

'Got to keep your strength up for the big decision,' he said, handing her a paper packet.

They walked through the gates and along a path that led to the lake. A young father was helping his little boy to direct a remote-controlled speedboat on the water. Pigeons flapped around the path, searching for discarded crisps and crumbs.

They sat down on a seat beside the lake. A couple of young mothers walked past pushing prams, chatting non-stop about the problems of bringing up babies.

'Well?' Greg turned to look at Lindy. 'If it takes you so long to come to a decision. . .'

'I've made up my mind,' she said firmly. 'It was something Ann Gregson said the other day. She said it was better to have loved and lost than never to have loved at all. Apparently she had a love affair years ago, and although it didn't work out she was glad she'd had the wonderful experience.'

She saw the puzzled look cross his face.

'Lindy, we've got each other now. We haven't split up.'

'But we both know that there's always a chance that we might split up. If I can't give you children, I won't hold you in the marriage,' she said quietly. 'And if we did split up I'd say it had been worth it. So, if you ask me one more time, I think you might stand a chance of being accepted.' She put down her half-eaten beef-burger.

Greg smiled. 'You're a difficult woman.'

Screwing up the paper from his burger and tossing it in the bin, he knelt down on the stony path and took hold of her hands.

Lindy was holding back her laughter as she watched the surrounding, crumb-eating pigeons scatter in all directions.

'These birds can be witness to the fact that I'm making a serious proposal,' Greg said. 'Lindy, will you marry me?'

'Yes.'

He breathed an exaggerated sigh of relief as he got up from his knees. 'Let's go back to the hotel and order some champagne. This calls for a celebration.'

He pulled her to her feet, wrapping her in his arms.

'I'd like to pick you up and carry you all the way back to the hotel, but maybe I'd better save my strength.'

He swept her out through the park gates and hailed a taxi.

The room Greg had reserved was spacious and luxurious. Lindy walked through into the bathroom to admire the gold taps adorning the Jacuzzi.

'Never been in a personal Jacuzzi before,' she said.

'You'll need a personal guide then,' he said, arriving at the bathroom door, wrapped in a white towelling robe.

Gently he removed the jacket of her suit, tossing it back into the bedroom.

There was a knock on the bedroom door. Lindy finished undressing in the bathroom while Greg dealt with the champagne that had just arrived. She heard the popping of the cork as she eased herself into the effervescent Jacuzzi.

'Room for one more in there?' Greg slipped into

the water beside her and handed her a bubbling glass of champagne.

Lindy found the contrast of the cold champagne and the warm Jacuzzi invigorating. The only blot on the landscape was the prospect that she might have to suffer more miscarriages or medically advised terminations. She would go through with it when the time came, and she would make a determined effort to stop worrying about it. For the moment she was floating on cloud nine.

She closed her eyes to savour the moment. Her toes were curling at the prospect of spending a whole night with Greg. His bare leg brushed hers in the water. She opened her eyes.

'Do you want some more champagne?' he asked, his voice husky with passion.

She shook her head languidly.

'Well, in that case, put down your glass and let's make love before all these bubbles drive me to distraction.'

He pulled her towards him, caressing her skin, running his fingers lightly over her breasts, exploring every part of her as they clung together in the warm, scented water. And when he entered her she cried out as the sensual excitement reached an impossible crescendo. He held her tightly against his muscular chest as the electric waves of passion rocked her to a climax.

She lay back in the water, panting for breath, her body still vibrating with waves of pleasure. She couldn't imagine that their lovemaking would ever be more exciting than now. She would never regret living with this man, however things turned out in the end.

Her only regret was the element of chance over starting a family, but then, Greg had said that nothing was ever certain in this world, so she would go along with that. She would live for the moment as long as it lasted.

'Penny for them,' he whispered.

'Just thinking about our future,' she said.

He reached for the champagne bottle and topped up their glasses.

'Let's drink to it,' he said, raising his glass to hers. 'To our future together.'

'For as long as it lasts,' Lindy said quietly.

She saw the flickering in his eyes as their glasses touched with a loud clinking sound.

'For as long as it lasts,' he repeated.

CHAPTER ELEVEN

As THE taxi from Moortown station reached the hospital the following evening Lindy felt some of her euphoria evaporating.

She waited until Greg had paid the driver.

'I need to check whether there are any important messages that need dealing with,' Greg said, turning round and walking with her towards the main entrance. 'If everything's OK we'll drive out to the pink house and have another celebration.'

'Greg, let's not announce our engagement yet. There's no hurry to set a date for the wedding and—'

'You've got cold feet, having second thoughts,' he said. 'It happens to everybody when they've got a big change in their lives looming ahead. You'll be OK when you've had a good night's sleep and—'

'No, Greg, seriously, I don't want to announce it yet.'

They were standing in front of the enquiries desk. Greg took her arm and steered her along the corridor towards the residents' quarters.

'Go and change into something relaxing and I'll pick you up as soon as—'

'I'm going up to Nightingale to check on my patients,' Lindy said quietly. 'I need to get on with my own life for a while. Please don't ask me why I feel like this because I can't understand it myself. We were so happy together in London but now the real life has to start again.'

He stopped at the top of the staircase and turned her round towards him.

'I won't pressure you into setting a date,' he said. 'We can still be together without any formal announcement if that's what you want.'

'It is,' she said quickly.

'OK,' he said in a subdued voice. 'Have you decided to stay here tonight?'

She nodded, her eyes searching his face. He was right when he said she'd got cold feet about marriage. There was so much at stake, so much uncertainty about their future together. If only she could look into the future and see whether or not. . .

'See you tomorrow,' he said, bending his head to kiss her on the cheek.

She skipped lightly down the steps without looking back. Her room was in the same chaos that she'd left it in. She spent a few minutes tidying up before having a quick shower and dressing in a thin cotton dress and white coat.

Sister Gregson was giving her day report to the night staff who were taking over when she arrived. She looked up from the counter of the nurses' station and smiled.

'Didn't expect you back this evening, Dr Cash. Did you have a good time?'

Lindy smiled back. 'Yes, thank you. I wanted to check on my patients.'

'Of course. Everything's quiet at the moment, but if you need anything Staff Nurse will help you.' She turned back to the night staff. 'Now, as I was saying, nurses, I want you to be absolutely sure that. . .'

Lindy walked down the ward, hearing Sister's strident voice exhorting her nurses to take meticulous care of their newest prem.

She went into the prem unit. The lights had been dimmed but monitors flashed out their messages beside the special cots. She checked on the charts, bringing herself up to date. The prem unit staff nurse, waiting to be relieved by the night staff, assured Lindy that there were no problems. The newest prem was holding his own and expected to be out of danger by morning.

Lindy went through to the mothers and babies unit, and for about an hour she walked between the beds, chatting to the mothers, setting their minds at rest where necessary, cuddling the babies, helping with feeds.

James Dewhirst came on the ward.

'Didn't expect to see you back this evening,' he said.

As she discussed the patients with him she realised that no one had expected her back. It hadn't been necessary for her to come in at all. She'd invented the excuse to get away from Greg. She'd deliberately turned him down. She was going to spend the night in her poky little room when she could have been lying in Greg's arms in the four-poster. She could spend every night with him for as long as it lasted. Why on earth didn't she settle for that?

'I've got to go,' she told James breathlessly. 'I only called in for a brief round of the patients.'

He looked at her quizzically. 'Are you sure you're feeling all right, Lindy?'

'Never felt better!'

She hurried back down the darkened ward. As she passed Sister's office she heard a female giggle coming from inside followed by a muted, masculine guffaw.

'Dr Cash,' one of the night nurses called quietly, 'Sister Gregson asked if you'd see her in her office before you go.'

Lindy stopped. 'Sounds like she's got visitors. I was just on my way out so if it's not important. . .'

The swing-door was opening.

'Greg! Why are you here?' She felt her pulses racing

as she looked up at him in the half-light of the nurses'
station.

'Sister Gregson wants to see me in her office,' he
replied.

'Snap!' Lindy said. 'I wonder what she wants.'

'Sister said you were to go straight in,' the nurse said.

Greg's arm at the back of her waist unnerved her
as they went in through the door. She wanted to be
alone with him, to tell him that she was prepared to
go through whatever life threw at them if only they
could be together. The sooner they could get away
from the ward. . .

She was unprepared for the surprising scene—Sister
Gregson, minus her cap, her greying, originally auburn
hair loosely combed about her face, her apron folded
neatly on one of the chairs and her starched dress
unbuttoned at the neck. Sitting very close beside her
was a small, rather rotund man, with high-coloured
cheeks and deep-set eyes that were now twinkling as
they'd certainly not twinkled on the two occasions
when Lindy had been in his company. At the banquet
he'd been thoroughly displeased with the way she'd
contradicted him, and during the interview he'd looked
as if his face would have cracked if he smiled.

But he was smiling now!

'I'm sure you know Sir Jack Hamilton,' Sister
simpered.

'Call me Jack,' said the chairman of the board,
taking over the proceedings with his customary air of
leadership.

'Ann and I have got an announcement to make and
we'd like you two to be the first to hear it. Ann was
even younger than you, Lindy, when she started going
out with me, but she was a stubborn young girl. I
suppose I was a bit stubborn as well, but she was worse
than me!'

Sister Gregson gave Sir Jack a fond smile. 'Go on, get to the point, Jack.'

'Well, anyway, we lost touch with each other. I got married and Ann stuck with her career. My wife died five years ago. A couple of weeks ago I decided to invite Ann out for a meal and everything took off again. It was like we'd never been apart. Last night I asked her to marry me and she's agreed. You're both invited to the wedding next month.'

'But that's wonderful!' Lindy said.

At the same time Greg was saying, 'Marvellous! Absolutely marvellous!'

Lindy looked at Sister Gregson. 'And you only got together again a couple of weeks ago?'

Sister smiled. 'Remember that day I was talking to you about. . .you know. . .well, it was in my mind because Jack had phoned up the night before, and although I'd agreed I still wasn't sure.'

Lindy heard Greg give an exaggerated groan. 'I know another woman who can't make up her mind.'

'That's why I'm here,' Sir Jack said briskly. 'Ann and I were discussing you two this evening and we decided you'd procrastinated long enough. If you go on that way you'll drift apart and spend a lifetime with the wrong partner or with no partner at all.'

'It may be better to have loved and lost but it's far better to have loved and kept on loving,' Ann Gregson said shyly.

'That's what I think,' Greg said quietly. 'Thanks, Sister, Sir Jack.' He turned to shake the older man by the hand. 'I'm not allowed to make an announcement myself but if I can talk some sense into this stubborn woman you'll be the first to hear the news, sir.'

Sir Jack gave him a wry grin. 'Good luck! If she gives as spirited a performance as she gave at her interview, it won't be easy.'

Greg's arm was around her waist. She felt that if she resisted he would carry her. She was aware of Sir Jack and Ann Gregson smiling encouragingly as she went out through the door.

'Greg! Don't I get a say in this conspiracy?' she said as the door closed.

'Shh! You'll waken the patients. Wait till we get home.'

Home! What a lovely thought. The four-poster, a whole night together. She leaned into his encircling arm as they walked down the corridor. Night staff passed them in the corridor but Lindy didn't care. . . didn't even notice them, if the truth was known!

'You told me Ann Gregson had been talking about having loved and lost,' Greg said as they went out to the car park. 'At the time I thought it was a bit romantic for her. I expect she'll now be talking about love regained.'

'Shouldn't that be paradise regained?'

'Same thing, different words,' Greg said, pulling her against him in the car. 'I'm not going to let you go, you know. I'm not going through the best years of my life with the wrong partner.'

The car sprung to life and she lay back against the back of the seat, closing her eyes. Minutes later she was asleep.

The next thing she knew Greg was opening the car door, hauling her into his arms and carrying her over the threshold into the house.

'Don't worry. I'll do a repeat performance after we're married,' he said breathlessly as he climbed the stairs to the bedroom.

He laid her down on the crimson counterpane of the four-poster.

'You've made the bed!' she said, sweeping her hands

over the smooth silk that matched the curtains.

'I've got myself a daily help. I don't want my bride to have to work her poor little fingers to the bone when she comes home from the hospital, especially if she's pregnant.'

'But I'm not pregnant and I'm not your bride yet.'

'There's no problem in either case,' he said, lifting her bodily so that he could pull back the covers. 'Let's snuggle down here before we get to grips with the situation. First we'd better get you out of that white coat. . .now the dress. . .'

'Greg. . .?' she began tentatively, trying to quell the sensual shivers running down her spine as she felt Greg's naked skin pressed against her own. She wanted to have a rational discussion before they made love, but it would be difficult if she gave in to her feelings.

'When I was on the ward tonight I realised I wanted to be with you even if we were taking a chance. . .on having a family that is,' she said carefully. 'I know you've been through a divorce so marriage to you isn't as binding as it is to me but—'

'You're wrong!'

She looked up and saw his eyes held a tormented expression. 'Greg, I was only saying what—'

'This marriage. . .our marriage will be permanent. It will last for ever and ever, until one of us dies. You may have thought I sounded facetious when I said we should take a chance but I was absolutely sure of my own feelings. I simply wasn't sure about yours. Our marriage is going to work out because we're going to devote a whole lifetime to making it work.'

She felt his arms tightening around her as his physical need for her became patently obvious.

'Darling, can we postpone the discussion for a little while,' he whispered. 'I've been very patient but if I don't make love to you soon. . .'

'I thought you'd never ask,' she whispered as his caressing hands moved over her quivering skin. . .

She lay exhausted in his arms, looking up at the crimson canopy above her.

'So that's the first part of the agreement reached, isn't it?' he murmured. 'You're going to be my bride very soon. We'll set the date as early as we can make it. How about Cragdale Church?'

'Perfect!'

She had a mental image of the tiny church beside the river that ran through the village.

'Lucy and my mum and stepdad will come over. Have we got room for them to stay here?'

'Depends how soon we can get the wedding. I'd planned to begin decorating the nursery.'

'Oh, Greg! Let's not count our chickens.' She felt a moment of panic. 'Call me superstitious if you like, but I really think it would be tempting fate.'

He brushed his lips across her cheek. 'Whatever you say; and, darling, if you'd really rather not get pregnant then. . .'

'I know how much you want children, Greg, so—'

'I don't want to be selfish about this after all you've been through, but yes, it would make me very happy to start a family. So tell me truthfully how you feel about the idea.'

She lay back against the pillows, imagining a small boy with Greg's dark hair, running among the flowers in the garden of the pink house. She had to take a chance; she must never give up hope.

'If it's a boy shall we paint the house blue?' she asked quietly.

'Oh, darling! I love you so much.' He buried his face in her hair.

Moments later he raised his head. 'Does that mean

I can throw away the condoms?'

She smiled. 'If you do, we'd better decide quickly on a date for the wedding.'

'And we'd better start practising,' he whispered, pulling her against him again. 'You know what we tell all our patients in the clinic. Practice makes perfect. . .'

EPILOGUE

LINDY walked across the wet grass, picking her way between the primroses. She wanted to gather some of the wild daffodils near the hedge to put on the dining table.

A sleek black car was purring up the hill. She smiled as Greg turned into the drive, his tyres crunching on the gravel as he pulled to a halt.

'You're early!' she called, clutching the daffodils as she ran across the grass to meet him.

He caught her in his arms and kissed her tenderly on the lips.

'Are you sure you should be out here gathering flowers? It's only March, you know, and I don't want you to catch cold.'

'I won't catch a cold; I'm very fit.'

She leaned her head against his shoulder as they walked inside together.

'I came home to give you a hand with the dinner tonight. I'm not sure it was a good idea having a dinner party so soon after—'

He stopped in mid-sentence, his face lighting up at the sound of their baby crying.

'Shall I bring him down, Lindy?'

She nodded. 'He's ready for a feed. Greg, don't worry about tonight. All my favourite baby-doctors will be here—Simon, Hannah, Brad, Sara; what could possibly go wrong?'

Greg paused at the foot of the stairs. 'But whatever possessed you to invite Jack and Ann Hamilton?'

Lindy smiled. '*Sir* Jack, if you don't mind, Greg

and Lady Ann. I invited them because they've been so good to me. Ever since they moved into Cragdale last month they've kept popping in to see if I needed anything from the shops and so on. They've offered to babysit. Ann says she misses the babies since she left hospital and got married. She can't wait to get her hands on mine.'

'Ours,' he corrected, with a wry grin. 'Don't forget I had something to do with producing our son.'

She laughed. 'As if I ever could!'

'Talking of babysitting, Rona says she'd love to come and help out when she's off duty.'

From upstairs the wailing was increasing.

Greg ran up the stairs two at a time. When he returned with the baby she was sitting in her favourite chair by the fire. It was a low nursing chair that Greg had found in an antique shop. He'd had it re-covered and given it to her only days after she'd discovered that she was pregnant, on their wedding day way back in June.

Greg placed their son gently in her arms. The baby nuzzled his head against her breast and started feeding.

'We'll have to choose a name soon,' Greg said, his eyes tender as he watched his wife and son. 'He's two weeks old and he'll have to have a name before he goes to Cragdale Primary School.'

Lindy laughed. 'We'll go over the list again tonight. How about Jonathan?'

'No, I prefer Michael, or how about Simon? That would please your obstetrician. Or we could—'

'If he'd been a girl it would have been easier. There are lots of names I like,' Lindy interrupted.

'Better save them. We may have a girl next time.'

Lindy picked up a cushion with her spare hand and aimed it at Greg's head.

'I thought you told me it was as easy as shelling peas,' he said as he ducked.

She smiled. 'It was. I never thought—' She broke off in mid-sentence, a faraway expression in her eyes.

He moved across and knelt down on the carpet, putting his arms around his wife and baby son.

'Never thought what, Lindy?' he prompted gently.

She'd been going to say that'd she never thought she would have a pregnancy and birth that would be totally free of complications, considering her obstetric problems in the past. But that was all history now. She'd put the past firmly behind her.

'I never thought I could be so happy,' she whispered.

Greg's arms tightened around them both as he kissed her.

GET 4 BOOKS AND A MYSTERY GIFT

Return this coupon and we'll send you 4 Medical Romances and a mystery gift absolutely FREE! We'll even pay the postage and packing for you.

We're making you this offer to introduce you to the benefits of Reader Service: FREE home delivery of brand-new Medical Romances, at least a month before they are available in the shops, FREE gifts and a monthly Newsletter packed with information.

Accepting these FREE books and gift places you under no obligation to buy, you may cancel at any time, even after receiving just your free shipment. Simply complete the coupon below and send it to:

MILLS & BOON READER SERVICE, FREEPOST, CROYDON, SURREY, CR9 3WZ.

No stamp needed

Yes, please send me 4 free Medical Romances and a mystery gift. I understand that unless you hear from me, I will receive 4 superb new titles every month for just £2.10* each postage and packing free. I am under no obligation to purchase any books and I may cancel or suspend my subscription at any time, but the free books and gifts will be mine to keep in any case. (I am over 18 years of age)

1EP6D

Ms/Mrs/Miss/Mr _____

Address _____

_____

_____ Postcode _____

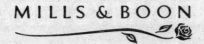

MILLS & BOON

MEDICAL ROMANCE
LOVE ON CALL

The books for enjoyment this month are:

TENDER TOUCH	Caroline Anderson
LOVED AND LOST	Margaret Barker
THE SURGEON'S DECISION	Rebecca Lang
AN OLD-FASHIONED PRACTICE	Carol Wood

Treats in store!

Watch next month for the following absorbing stories:

A PRIVATE AFFAIR	Sheila Danton
DOCTORS IN DOUBT	Drusilla Douglas
FALSE PRETENCES	Laura MacDonald
LOUD AND CLEAR	Josie Metcalfe

Available from W.H. Smith, John Menzies, Volume One,
Forbuoys, Martins, Woolworths, Tesco, Asda, Safeway and
other paperback stockists.

Readers in South Africa - write to:
IBS, Private Bag X3010, Randburg 2125.